Minuet at Midnight

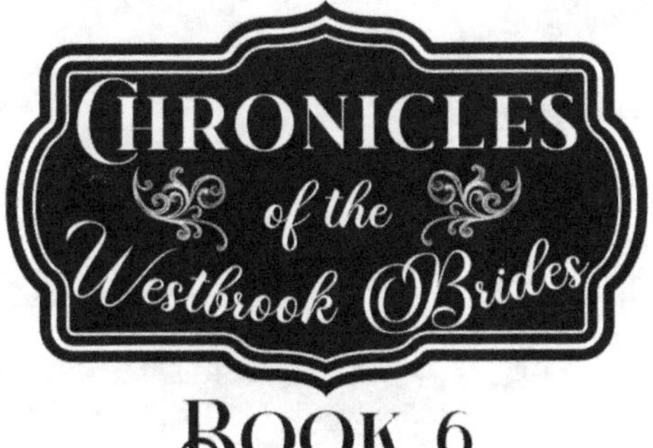

BOOK 6

USA Today Bestselling Author

COLLETTE CAMERON®

SWEET-TO-SPICY TIMELESS ROMANCE®

Blue Rose Romance® LLC

Leonidas
gave her
a wicked wink.

"One of these days,
I vow,
I'm going to
have that
kiss..."

USA Today Bestselling Author
Sweet to Spicy Timeless Romance®
COLLETTE
collettecameron.com
CAMERON®
Blue Rose Romance® LLC

PRAISE FOR...
MINUET AT MIDNIGHT©

See What Readers Are Saying About
Minuet at Midnight!

★ ★ ★ ★ ★ "Wonderful characters, excellent story and romance all wrapped in one."

— LISA C

★ ★ ★ ★ ★ "The story flowed effortlessly & I devoured this utterly charming romance in a sitting. I just love the Westbrook family."

— JANET

★ ★ ★ ★ ★ "Okay, this book actually made me cry when it got close to the end. It's been so long since a book has brought that out in me, but one scene between Leonidas and Primrose touched my heart to the point where it brought tears. A good book will make you laugh; a great book will make you cry."

— K. HUDECEK

★ ★ ★ ★ ★ "I didn't realize how connected I had become to Primrose and Leonidas until I found myself crying in the third act."

— SANDRA W.

★ ★ ★ ★ ★ "Ms. Cameron has woven a heartwarming story...The classic, quirky Cameron banter and dialogue will have you laughing out loud and enjoying every moment of the book. I cannot wait for the next book and more family intrigue!!"

— TERRIE

MINUET AT MIDNIGHT

ROMANTIC OPPOSITES ATTRACT MYSTERY &
SUSPENSE FAMILY SAGA REGENCY ROMANCE

CHRONICLES OF THE WESTBROOK BRIDES
BOOK SIX

COLLETTE CAMERON®

GET YOUR FREE BOOK!
THE REGENCY ROSE®

JOIN MY EXCLUSIVE MAILING LIST
AND GET A FREE EBOOK!

Plus Sneak Peeks, Giveaways, Contests,
Exclusive Content and More...
P.S. I promise only good stuff ~ no spammy stuff!

Scan the following QR Code to join
The Regency Rose VIP Group Mailing List
and get your FREE BOOK!

Thank you,
Collette Cameron®

THE
REGENCY
ROSE®
VIP
CLUB

*For every reader who stays up way too late
reading just one more page.*

ONE

West India Docks
London, England

MAY 1827 – LATE AFTERNOON

Long shadows stretched their wispy, slightly eerie fingers along the bustling wharf as the surprisingly clean and well-maintained hackney rumbled over the sturdy pier. Sailors, laborers, merchants, and others scurried here and there, dashing in front of carts or maneuvering their way around laden wagons, crates, and barrels.

After over a week of hard traveling and constantly looking over her shoulder, Primrose McKessick had reached her destination. Safe at last, she exhaled a long, shaky breath.

Today was the beginning of her new life—a much better life, she prayed.

Sulky clouds hung low in the sky, promising more rain.

What was a little rain to a Scot?

Accustomed to the dock's commotion, mangy dogs and scraggly cats darted between stacked goods and vehicle wheels. Bedraggled street urchins with hungry eyes and gaunt faces covertly searched for an easy pocket to pick, and what Primrose suspected were prostitutes hawking their wares flirted outrageously with any man who passed them.

The hired hack proved no protection from the busy pier's hubbub and din or the tangy air, tinged with sea and sewage, assailing her nostrils.

Primrose scanned the crumpled, short, rather sloppily written letter from her great maternal aunt as she'd done at least a hundred times in the past ten days as she raced from the Highlands to London.

The instructions were clear.

Meet Aunt Rhodesia Shenton-Wayford at West India Docks on the second of May at half-four to board the sailing vessel *Sea Queen* for an extended holiday in Italy as her paid companion.

Thank God for Aunt Rhodesia's benevolence and

kindness and the fortuitous timing of her trip. The poor dear had penned the letter to Primrose as Aunt Rhodesia recovered from a sprained wrist resulting from a tumble over a footstool.

Had Aunt Rhodesia not extended the offer, Primrose might have found herself on the street or forced to become the third wife of feudal baron Wallace MacLerie, Baron of Glentorquith.

Lyster McKessick arranged the marriage of convenience after accepting MacLerie's two-hundred-pound bribe and informing Primrose she could no longer live or work at his establishment. Never a loving father, his cold dispassion as he kicked her to the curb still took her aback, nonetheless.

Primrose wrinkled her nose and pursed her lips.

She'd been bought and paid for like a pair of plow horses and given no choice about the match.

Had Lyster truly believed she'd comply without a fight?

Primrose wasn't the quiet, docile, defeated woman Mama had become. No indeed. She'd have joined the Black Tinkers roaming Scotland and lived a gypsy's life before submitting to his drunken demands.

Sagging against the charcoal-gray squabs, Primrose permitted an exuberant smile as she roved her gaze over the two tattered and stuffed valises across from her. They contained all that she owned in the world. Perhaps not much by some people's standards, but plenty for her to start over in England.

For as long as she drew breath, she never intended to return to her homeland.

There was no reason to now, in any event.

Not only had she fooled the man the world falsely believed was her father—Mama had told Primrose the ugly truth at the tender age of five to explain McKessick's ongoing cruelty—but she'd also finally escaped MacLerie's lustful clutches.

And now, Primrose was to set off on a grand adventure, the likes of which she'd never have dared to dream.

Perhaps Mama was right.

Every cloud contained a silver lining—if you but looked for it.

Gulls' raucous cries interrupted her introspection and dragged her back to the present.

Spain. Italy. Greece.

Six months of traveling—something she'd always yearned to do but never hoped to experience. Seeing exotic places. Eating unfamiliar food. Enjoying unusual customs. Surely McKessick and MacLerie would've given up searching for her by then—if they even bothered to in the first place.

A lazy *skellum*, McKessick probably wouldn't inconvenience himself.

MacLerie, on the other hand, very well might.

Accustomed to using intimidation and bribery to get his way, the man didn't take *no* for an answer. That's why she had traveled under the plain, unremarkable, and forgettable assumed name of Joane Porter.

Primrose might only be two inches over five feet tall, but she possessed spirit.

Mama always said so.

"Primrose Crystabel Faye, how does such a small form contain so much fortitude, resilience, and tenacity, my darling girl?"

Hadn't Primrose managed to outsmart those two tosspots?

Indeed, she had, though she could well imagine their rage at having been thwarted.

She winced at the thought, a chill racing up her spine and leaving goose pimples on her arms. With a gossamer-thin grasp on sanity and given to blood-curdling threats and malevolent violence, McKessick and MacLerie were men she hoped never to encounter again.

Primrose's earlier exuberance flitted away as the other reason for her hasty, secretive departure from her birth-place forced its ugly head into her gleeful musings.

Last month, the frail body of her only surviving sibling, dear, sweet, sickly Oleander, finally succumbed to the myriad of ailments that had plagued him since his birth twelve years ago. She'd nursed him to the best of her ability, but it hadn't been enough. His death sent Lyster into a drunken binge, leaving Primrose to make the burial arrangements.

Oleander died a mere three months after Mama passed while giving birth to yet another stillborn child. In all, Rosmund Tierney McKessick, the once-pampered youngest daughter of an English viscount, had suffered six miscarriages and three stillbirths.

Every instance since she turned ten, Primrose had assisted Mama with the aftermath, begging her to stay in bed and rest so her worn-out body could recover.

Usually soused to the gills by noon, Lyster—the inconsiderate, worse-than-a-rutting-bull brute—would rage and swear at poor Mama for failing him once more. Before her body could recover, he'd be on her again like flies on a carcass. *Inconsiderate beast.* The tippler blamed her for losing the other children and resented Primrose's health and vigor.

Sudden grief-born tears welled in her eyes, but she blinked them away with furious determination.

Not today.

Today was a day to celebrate, not mourn. She would never again feel Lyster's hand upon her cheek, wrenching her arm, or yanking her hair. Never again would she suffer his foul curses and raving rants bordering on lunacy.

And, praise God and all the saints, never again would she have to suffer MacLerie's *accidental* caresses and lecherous ogling while she served him in *The Quacking Dog,*

Lyster's tavern and inn, where she'd labored for free since she could lift a broom and wipe a table.

The inn was supposed to have been named *The Quaking Dog*—more of Lyster's perverse humor—but the painter misspelled the word, and the unfortunate name had stuck, even after Lyster had ripped the sign down and stomped it to pieces.

He hadn't paid her for her labor, but Primrose had saved and hidden the tips secretly slipped to her by sympathetic patrons over the years. Those carefully secreted away coins had made this escape possible. She'd chosen to use these unforeseen circumstances to forge what she hoped would be a happy future.

Attitude and outlook are everything, Mama used to admonish softly.

Both the youngest children of nobles, Mama had remained good, sweet, and kind while Lyster embodied all that was selfish, abhorrent, and foul in humanity.

The hack slowed to a rocky stop, and the vehicle bounced as the lanky driver descended.

Primrose's stomach pitched from excitement and nerves. She'd barely tucked the letter into her reticule and adjusted her plain straw bonnet when the door swung open.

"Here you are, miss."

His lean face creased into a toothy smile, reminding her of the brown hares hopping through the fields at home. The jarvey extended his hand, treating Primrose like a proper lady instead of the by-blow of the married lord who'd raped her mother over two decades ago.

Mama never told Primrose who her father was, only that he'd been older, married, and taken her virtue by force. Oh, and that he'd died from a wound received on the field of honor a couple of years later after despoiling a duke's daughter.

No one in Mama's family had protected her honor as fervently as that unnamed duke had defended his daughter's, hence Mama's hasty and reluctant marriage to Lyster—the only man who would have her.

His copper-brown eyes alight with kindness, the driver assisted Primrose from the conveyance before reaching inside, retrieving her bags, and setting them near her dusty and worn half boots.

"The ship be just yonder." He angled his bony chin toward a majestic vessel with her crew busily preparing for departure.

"Thank you." She arched her spine, stiff from so many days of sitting.

A small frisson of uncertainty trailed across her shoulders.

Where was Aunt Rhodesia?

A frown furrowed the driver's high forehead.

"Ain't no one meetin' ye?"

TWO

❧◉❧

Pushing his cap back, the driver glanced around, his concern palpable. "The docks ain't no place for an unaccompanied lady."

"Yes, my aunt is meeting me." Primrose searched again for Aunt Rhodesia's familiar face. "We're sailing with the tide."

Two coaches, one bearing a gleaming crest and from which numerous crates and trunks had been unloaded and stacked on the dock, lay parked several feet farther down the crowded pier.

"Ye did say the *Sea Queen*?" The hackney driver removed his flat cap and after scratching his head and cramming the accessory back on his bald pate, he gestured toward the ship halfway between the hackney and the coaches.

"Yes." Of that, Primrose was certain.

She passed him a few coins, though she couldn't spare them. He'd been so kind and helpful, however. And after today, she wouldn't have to scrimp and save every penny anymore.

"Thank ye, kindly, miss."

Hands thrust in his trouser pockets, he took up a position a few feet away, making it apparent that he acted as her protector.

"I'll just wait with ye, miss."

At the speculative glances a few of the bolder men on the pier cast in her direction, Primrose couldn't ignore the slight tremor skittering up her spine. After working in Lyster's hostelry for over fifteen years, she ought to be as used to leering men as she was to ribald speech and bawdy jokes. Still, she gave the hack driver a grateful smile, welcoming his presence and appreciating his thoughtfulness.

A cat raced across the scarred wooden pier, a scruffy dog yapping in pursuit. Farther along the other end of the wharf, a bewhiskered gentleman assisted a stout lady up a gangway. A manservant and what must be a lady's maid trailed behind, bearing their luggage.

Rotating her neck to ease the tightness there, Primrose swept her attention up and down the pier.

Where was Aunt Rhodesia?

A plump man in a leaf-brown striped suit bustled around the front of the unmarked coach and, appearing disgruntled with his hands on his hips, surveyed the wharf. Upon spotting her standing uncertainly, a grin split his face, and he marched forward, his rotund belly leading the way like a plow before a horse.

"Primrose!" he hailed from several feet away. "It *is* you."

"Cousin Chesley?"

She peered behind him for Aunt Rhodesia and her lady's maid. Perhaps they waited in the coach or had already boarded the vessel. "Am I late?"

"Not a bit of it." Face flushed and his cheeks mottled red, he shifted his mossy-brown eyes here and there, unable—*or unwilling*—to meet her gaze straight on. He darted his tongue out and licked his upper lip.

Like a great toad.

Primrose couldn't regret her uncharitable comparison. Particularly as his unfortunate choice of a green waistcoat and absence of a noticeable neck reinforced the comparison.

"Shall we?" Still grinning, he extended his arm in the *Sea Queen's* general direction. Beads of perspiration dotted his upper lip and brow, and telltale dampness darkened his jacket beneath his arms, though it wasn't overly warm outside.

Aunt Rhodesia hadn't mentioned Chesley would travel with them, though Primrose supposed as her only son, it made sense. Nevertheless, a twinge of disappointment pricked her, and she had to remind herself that she was at Aunt Rhodesia's mercy and munificence.

Regardless, Primrose held no fondness for Chesley.

Spoiled rotten by his doting mother, he'd been unkind to her the few times they'd met as children, secretly pulling her hair and pinching her, though he was ten years her senior. He also lied constantly, often blaming her for his nasty antics.

From opposite ends, another pair of men rounded the waiting coaches—one tall and well-built and the other squat and broad. The first, with a dove gray hat atop midnight hair and his tailored ash-gray coat, reminded Primrose of a sleek greyhound.

In contrast, the second fellow, with his wide shoulders, thick neck, meaty face, and attired in a tan jacket and buff-colored pantaloons, more closely resembled a bulldog.

She concealed a grin.

The unfortunate but amusing childhood habit of occasionally comparing people to dogs entertained her.

As he had as a child, Chesley still resembled an obese pug with bad teeth and fetid breath.

Head tilted upward, the taller man spoke to the driver, unfastening luggage from the back of the coach bearing the crest, while the shorter, muscled fellow leaned against Aunt Rhodesia's coach with his arms folded.

Who was the latter chap, and why was he here?

He wasn't Aunt Rhodesia's coachman.

That ancient servant dozed in the driver's seat, his chin on his chest.

The hackney driver quirked a brow, silently asking if all was well.

"This is my cousin." She nodded to reassure him. "I shall be fine. I appreciate your consideration."

"My pleasure, miss." After putting two fingers to his forehead, the jarvey clambered aboard the hack and drove away.

Chesley had waddled ten feet farther down the pier. Since the last time she'd seen him, he'd put on a good stone—or four. A frown dragged his untamed eyebrows together over his beak-like nose.

"Are you coming, Primrose?"

Impatience and something slightly more sinister tinged his whiny voice.

The rotter didn't even offer to carry one of her bags.

So typical of cossetted and coddled Chesley—Aunt Rhodesia's one shortfall. Blinded by love for her son, she could never see his flaws, of which there were too many to count.

"Yes. Of course." With a little grunt, Primrose lifted her heavy bags and plodded forward.

Instead of directing her toward the gangplank, Chesley marched toward the coach.

A wave of unease tripped along her shoulders.

"Hasn't Aunt Rhodesia already boarded the ship?" she asked.

"*Pardon*?" Chesley half-turned, his face a mask of irritation. His expression cleared, and he shook his head. "No. No. There's been a slight change of plans."

He chuckled, a placating, artificial gurgle that raised her nape hairs.

"*Change of plans*? What sort of change of plans?"

Ten feet from Aunt Rhodesia's coach, Primrose slowed to a stop.

Again, unease warned her something wasn't as it should be.

The man in gray tossed her a cursory glance as he accepted a box from his driver. He possessed the bluest eyes she'd ever seen, fringed by thick, sooty lashes.

They rivaled the Highland summer sky or Loch Ness in June.

"Yes. Dear Mama mixed up the sailing date." Chesley held the coach door open. "The ship sails the day after tomorrow. She bids me fetch you home and apologizes that she did not come herself. Her arthritis is acting up."

Probably worse in her injured wrist.

Out of breath from trying to keep up, Primrose glanced toward her aunt's coach.

The bulldog man with muddy brown eyes had straightened and now examined her from head to toe with the intensity a cook might while selecting a prime piece of meat for supper.

Something definitely wasn't right.

Not right at all.

Though Chesley's story was plausible, warning bells clanged loudly in her ears.

Leaving her bags, she approached the tall stranger. "Excuse me, sir?"

What had she to lose with her daring?

Nothing, and much to gain if her intuition proved correct.

She would learn whether Chesley—a habitual liar—told the truth, and every womanly instinct she possessed shouted that he fibbed. Curiously, those same premonitions also assured her she could trust the striking man in gray.

Either her instincts were spot on, or she was in a bumblebroth up to her neck.

"*Prim—rose.*" Chesley fairly growled, dragging her name out several syllables and pitching his voice high at the end. "Stop dawdling. *Get* into the coach."

The blue-eyed man turned, and she was quite certain he assessed her thoroughly in a heartbeat before skimming his cool gaze over Chesley and the bulldog.

"Yes, miss? May I be of assistance?"

He possessed a lovely voice, deep and rich like velvet.

No annoyance or irritation etched his face or threaded his tone, but rather an unexpected but wholly welcome sincerity.

"Primrose," Chesley snapped, all pretense at civility gone. "Mother *is* waiting. She shall become worried should we delay any longer. Don't bother this gentleman with your silliness."

"'Tis no bother to assist the lady." Flintiness entered the gentleman's eyes and voice.

His massive drivers descended from the coach and placed themselves on either side of him, expressing without words that they were there to defend him.

Who was he?

A gentleman, to be sure.

Likely a lord, given the coach's crest.

The bulldog had the unmitigated gall to approach her, his demeanor menacing and his oily, reptilian eyes sending an icy shudder up her spine.

"Better do as your cousin asks, Miss McKessick. You wouldn't wish for your aunt to fret, now would you? It is going to rain soon too."

Stiffening, Primrose retreated two paces.

How dare he address her, let alone presume to tell her what to do?

They hadn't been introduced.

More unnerving, however, was why Chesley had revealed her name to a seedy stranger?

Furthermore, Scotswomen were well accustomed to rain.

Resisting the urge to hide behind the tall, blue-eyed figure just a few feet away regarding her with unexpected but appreciated patience, Primrose pointed toward the *Sea Queen* instead.

"I'm sorry to bother you, sir. But when does this ship sail, and where does she sail to?"

The handsome stranger puzzled his noble forehead before veering a sideways glance toward Chesley and the bulldog. He swept his keen gaze over her once more.

"The *Sea Queen* sails to Greece on the evening tide."

THREE

TEN DISTRESSING SECONDS LATER

Leonidas Westbrook silently signaled his coachmen to be vigilant. The petite young woman's hazel-blue eyes beneath winged dark blond eyebrows went wide and then narrowed in dismay.

"*Greece*?" she whispered, shaking her head while backing away from the exasperated men demanding she enter the other coach. "*Not* Italy?"

Instantly alert, Leonidas took in her shock and fear, her cousin's increasing agitation, and the other man's irritated impatience.

What went on here?

Nothing above board, that was certain.

Her well-modulated speech held the merest hint of Scots brogue, though no one in the most elite drawing rooms could fault her English accent. She had the bearing and poise of a noblewoman, but her humble attire suggested common origins.

"Aye." Leonidas grasped his lapel with one hand while sliding his other into his jacket pocket, where a custom-made, bone-handled knife with a razor-sharp pivoting blade lay nestled.

"The toff is mistaken, Primrose." Her cousin took two steps forward but froze when Baldwin, the larger of the Duke of Latham's drivers, made a threatening noise in his throat.

At eighteen stone and five inches over six feet, Baldwin had made a living in the ring for several years before Father had persuaded him to come to work for him. Farrel, the other coachman and Baldwin's younger brother, could wield a sword with as much skill as he did his ham-like fists.

Leonidas curved his mouth into a mocking smile. "This *toff* has booked passage on the ship, so I believe I know where I am sailing to. The *Sea Queen* most assuredly sails to Greece, *not* Italy."

After a year and a half in England, Leonidas had finally arranged for another adventure, intending to write his fifth traveling book. He'd never planned on staying in

England this long, but his half-brother Fletcher's issues with his clubs and ongoing threats he refused to share with the rest of the Westbrooks had kept Leonidas at home much longer than expected. Those problems had diminished in recent weeks, and now Leonidas felt he could leave without fretting about Fletcher's wellbeing.

Besides, had he left sooner, he would've missed Adolphus's, Lucius's, and Althelia's weddings. He couldn't be more pleased that his sister had married his best friend. He rather felt like Cupid must after successfully arranging a love match. Though truth be told, it never occurred to Leonidas that Owen Lockington would fall in love with his unconventional sister.

That only left Cassius and Darius to march down the aisle.

For, like himself, his older half-brothers Layton and Fletcher, were avowed bachelors. Layton had been married several years ago, but no one spoke about that disaster. Once burned, he was not the least interested in repeating that mistake.

"I told you, Primrose. Mother made a mistake with the ships and dates." Shifting his feet, her cousin patted the coach's side. "Let's go home and sort it out, shall we?"

The aged driver continued to doze atop the coach, oblivious to the scene playing out below him. The poor fellow ought to have retired years ago.

Dread and suspicion skittered across Miss McKessick's

pretty features. She pressed her Cupid's bow mouth into a thin ribbon, two lines appearing on the bridge of her nose. Distrust fairly radiated off her in undulating waves, so potent Leonidas felt them from where he stood.

A peculiar urge to wrap an arm around her shoulders and comfort her engulfed him. He summed up the mysterious impulse as compassion for a frightened creature.

He returned to studying the belligerent men demanding she go with them.

The muscled brute seemed vaguely familiar, but Leonidas couldn't recall how he knew the fellow.

The other chap he didn't recognize.

"Aunt Rhodesia isn't going to Italy, is she?" Stricken and pale as the fichu tucked into her bodice, Miss Primrose McKessick swallowed.

Leonidas had gleaned her name from the blackguards ordering her around.

"I'd vow she didn't write and ask me to accompany her either." Her skin had acquired a waxen tone, but she held herself with a soldier's discipline. "She doesn't even know I'm coming, does she?"

The motley flush reddening her cousin's face answered her question and validated Leonidas's concern.

This pair was up to no good, for certain.

She pointed a shaking finger at the stout man, now fairly frothing with wrath. "*You* impersonated Aunt Rhodesia and wrote the letter, Chesley. But why?"

"*Harumph.*" The driver awoke with a start, and confusion pleated his face into scores of deep lines as he looked from person to person.

Sudden recognition slammed into Leonidas, accompanied by good measures of disgust and disbelief, and he squelched a foul oath. He realized who the shorter chap was. Fletcher had pointed him out one afternoon as the coach bore them through a seedier part of London.

Mother of God.

If this woman had entered that coach...

Leonidas couldn't finish the thought.

Even more disturbing and unforgivable, the younger, fat-as-a-hog fellow was her cousin.

What a reprehensible maggot—an irredeemable reprobate and waste of humanity.

Leonidas stepped forward, placing himself between the distraught woman and the men determined to hie off with her.

"I believe I can satisfactorily answer that, Miss McKessick."

She tore her dismayed gaze away from the ominous men but only long enough to send Leonidas an inquisitive glance that seemed to say, "*Well, get on with it then. Explain it to me.*"

He exchanged a telling look with his coachmen, and the merest flexing of the outer corners of their eyes and almost indecipherable nods indicated they understood.

Be prepared to fight.

Father insisted his coachmen were always armed as well as being expert pugilists. One never knew when the duke or his family might need protection. Or, in this case, when a damsel in distress might require assistance.

Leonidas best make haste, however.

His luggage still sat on the pier, and he preferred to unpack before the ship pulled anchor with the evening tide. Another vessel didn't sail to Greece for several weeks; this night, he intended to stand at the rail and watch England's shoreline fade from view.

Positive his drivers would defend Miss McKessick, Leonidas canted his head and speared the thick-necked man a contemptuous glance. His stomach coiled, and anger tunneled through his veins when he realized what these men had intended for the girl.

Making no attempt to hide his scorn, Leonidas pinned the scowling flesh peddler with a murderous glare.

"You are Gilroy Hadleigh, otherwise known as the West End Whoremaster. I'd wager you have an arrangement with this ponce," he flicked a finger at Chesley who was dragging a sodden handkerchief over his sweaty, blotchy face, "to provide you with innocents for your brothels."

Hadleigh's whorehouses were notorious for being the foulest in England. Prostitutes rarely lived a year after the Whoremaster sank his cruel talons into them.

God rot the despicable sod, and may he burn in hell.

"*Guid Laird, nae!*" Gasping, her face ravaged by horror, Miss McKessick stumbled backward several paces, clutching a hand to her throat. Anger thickened her brogue.

"Chesley Shenton-Wayford, ye'd sell yer own flesh and blood to a...a..." She struggled to find the right word. "A *drùisear? A pimp?*"

Making a distressed sound in his throat, the elderly coachman shook his head. He opened his mouth, but Shenton-Wayford shot him a quelling glower.

"It's not what you think, Primrose," her cousin cajoled, his tone wheedling. "I already explained. Mama mixed up the ships too. Sadly, she's become slightly addled in her old age."

"What a convenient excuse," Miss McKessick snapped. "I don't believe a word of it."

Good for you because the maggot-brain is lying through his crooked teeth.

"How do you explain *his* presence, Chesley? A known pimp?" Pointing at Hadleigh, she jutted her adorable rosebud of a chin upward, defiance sparking in her eyes. "Just a happy coincidence?"

Leonidas couldn't help but admire her fortitude and spirit. She transformed her fright and consternation into ire, and instead of cowering, she'd gone on the offense.

"Enough of this." Rage contorted Shenton-Wayford's

features, and he stomped forward, though he was dicked in the knob if he believed Leonidas would simply stand by and permit him to abscond with the girl.

"You're coming with us, Primrose. Everything has been arranged and cannot be undone."

I'll just bet it has been.

Chesley Shenton-Wayford was as stupid as a potato.

He'd essentially confessed to his part in the conspiracy to prostitute Miss McKessick.

Hadleigh shifted as if he, too, meant to seize her.

"I wouldn't." Leonidas withdrew his knife. Flicking the blade open, he simultaneously shoved Miss McKessick behind his back. "She's made it clear she's unwilling to go with you. Unless you intend to take her by force?" he mocked.

"You cannot stop us," Shenton-Wayford roared.

Like two demented, wild boars, he and Hadleigh charged forward. Perhaps they honestly believed the element of surprise would avail them a modicum of advantage or, perchance, they'd already accepted payments for providing a *new* girl tonight.

Some men would pay a small fortune to rape an innocent.

Baldwin and Farrel needed no prompting to render Shenton-Wayford and Hadleigh unconscious with well-placed facers. They sprawled on the ground, blood trickling from Hadleigh's cheek and Shenton-Wayford's mouth.

A long shadow fell across their prone forms, and Leonidas swung around, prepared to defend himself and Miss McKessick against the new arrival.

"Hold there, Cousin." Hands held upward to stave off an attack, Leonidas's cousin, Torrian Wyatt Westbrook, grinned at him. "I thought you might require assistance, but I should've known Uncle Haygarth's bodyguards would be up to the task."

Leonidas relaxed and pocketed the knife before shaking Torrian's hand. "Don't tell me you came to see me off?"

Shaking his head, Torrian chuckled.

"No. I'm waist-deep in an investigation, and my inquiries brought me to the docks." He lowered his voice so no one would overhear him. "In truth, I'm investigating the murders of several prostitutes, and I believe Hadleigh is involved. I've been tailing him for weeks, but he's a slimy devil. Always manages to slip away like the cockroach that he is."

Such relief swept Leonidas that Miss McKessick had been spared a life worse than death, and he slapped his cousin's shoulder. "Your timing is impeccable."

Torrian shifted his attention to Miss McKessick.

Eyeing her would-be abductors as one might plague-ridden corpses, she skirted their prone forms and retrieved her satchels.

"Playing the chivalrous hero these days, aye?" Torrian quipped. "Do you intend to write this interlude into your next book? Mayhap you've taken up writing gothic romance novels?"

His voice trembled with his mirth.

"Don't be an arse, Torrian. I could scarcely abandon her to their nefarious purposes."

Leonidas speared him a quelling glance before hurrying to Miss McKessick's side.

The large, rather tattered bags she clutched in either hand seemed as if they might topple her petite form should she lean too far to one side. She slowly roamed her dazed stare over the dockyard.

She reminded him of a scared puppy, though something told him she wouldn't appreciate the comparison.

"Miss McKessick?"

FOUR

Leonidas touched her arm when she didn't respond.

"Miss McKessick?"

Slowly, she angled her head and focused on him. "Yes?"

She truly was in a state of shock.

"Have you anywhere to go?" Leonidas asked with growing concern. She wasn't much younger than his sister, and the same protective instinct he'd always had for Althelia burgeoned behind his breastbone. "Is there anyone who might assist you?"

She blinked up at him, and to his utter horror, tears filled her hazel eyes.

"I...don't know." Once more searching the docks with a vacant stare, she shook her head. "The voyage was to have been my escape."

Her escape?

There was a tale there.

Leonidas was certain of it.

"I don't think I can intrude upon my aunt now," she said before capturing her quivering lower lip between small square teeth. "She doesn't know I'm in England, and after Chesley—"

No, that wouldn't do at all.

She must stay as far away from her villainous cousin as possible.

"Miss McKessick?" Shenton-Wayford's driver's thin, quavering voice drew Leonidas's and her attention. Shoulders slumped and the picture of remorse, the driver cleared his throat. "I didn't know what those blighters were about. I swear upon me mother's grave, God rest her soul."

Leonidas believed him.

"Your aunt died nearly five months ago. Mr. Shenton-Wayford owes money to dangerous men. He's sold everything of value, except this coach and team. You wouldn't be safe at the house." Eyes shadowed with worry and features stamped with regret, he shook his white head. "There's only me and the cook left—she's me wife."

"That's why Aunt Rhodesia never responded to my

letter informing her of Mama's death. I'll bet that's why Chesley is desperate for funds and would sell me. The rotter probably gambled away his inheritance already."

Leonidas couldn't refute her logic.

Peering off into space, Miss McKessick spoke to herself. "I should've known something was off, that this opportunity was too good to be true. Now what am I to do? I cannot go back to Scotland. *I cannot.*"

What had caused her to flee Scotland and refuse to return, especially given the current alarming situation?

Her lower lip trembled, but she bit it into submission again.

Leonidas sighed.

There was no help for it.

He wasn't sailing today.

What were a few more weeks after a year and a half?

He skimmed his focus over the two unconscious miscreants.

But *who* to give his passage to?

Shenton-Wayford or Hadleigh?

Torrian was investigating Hadleigh, so he would be under constant surveillance.

Shenton-Wayford it was then.

"Baldwin, you and Farrel carry Shenton-Wayford aboard the *Sea Queen*." Leonidas straightened his hat. "Inform the captain that the bugger is taking my passage. Offer the captain a nice bonus for his cooperation and discretion. Then please load my belongings back onto the coach."

He gave the drivers an apologetic smile. At least they didn't have to offload Orion from the ship. Though it had been a difficult decision and he'd miss the horse, Leonidas had left his favorite mount at Hefferwickshire House. It wasn't fair to make the animal endure ocean voyages below deck.

"Yes, my lord." Baldwin nodded before he and Farrel each wrapped one of Shenton-Wayford's arms around their necks and hauled him up the gangplank with the same care and courtesy as one might a carpet soiled with fresh horse manure.

"I'll take care of Hadleigh," Torrian offered, giving Miss McKessick an understanding smile. "It won't keep him off the streets for long, but it will give you enough time to see that she's safe, Leonidas. I have a man watching him 'round the clock."

"Thank you." Leonidas forced his lips upward. He faced Shenton-Wayford's frail driver. "You'd best be off. You don't want to get caught up in this mess."

"Aye, sir. I'm done, I am." He spat upon the ground, then speared Shenton-Wayford's back with a contemptuous glower. "That fat bugger hasn't paid me in three months. Me daughter has asked us to come live with her. That's where me wife and I are headed this very day."

"Good man." Leonidas nodded as he lifted a purse to

the man. "Take it. You've earned it. Enjoy your retirement."

"Thank you, my lord." A moment later, the coach trundled away.

That only left one question.

What was Leonidas going to do with Primrose McKessick?

As if reading his mind, Torrian asked, "What's to become of her?"

"I'll be hanged if I know." Leonidas pointed his attention skyward. "I suppose I must avail myself of Fletcher's hospitality, at least temporarily, until other arrangements can be made."

"Excellent notion. His army of bodyguards will assure her safety." Torrian gave a subtle signal, and four rough-looking men emerged from the pier's shadows. He spoke to them for a moment, and then they wordlessly piled Hadleigh into a nearby wagon and drove away with the cur.

"I'm off, Leonidas." Torrian shifted his focus to Miss McKessick. "I'll report in a few days."

Then, with a jaunty wave, he sauntered down the pier.

Miss McKessick focused her distracted gaze, now slate-colored with distress.

"Thank you for your assistance, sir."

She'd reverted to proper English.

As she pivoted away, her bags thumped against her calves and banged again with each step.

Where, for all the bloody tea in England, did she think she was going?

"Wait, Miss McKessick."

Glancing over her shoulder, she gave Leonidas a dubious look.

He hurried forward.

"My brother has an establishment a few streets away. He actually owns three, but *De la Chance* is the closest. It's a social club—gaming, entertainment, food, dancing, that sort of thing. No skullduggery or prostitutes," he rushed to assure her.

She didn't appear the least convinced, but who could blame her after what had just occurred?

"He's extremely selective about his clientele, and the establishment is very reputable." Fletcher believed his less desirable competitors had tried, unsuccessfully, to run him out of town. "You needn't fear for your honor or safety there, I assure you."

Indecision played across her features in the waning light.

What if she refused to go with him?

Leonidas couldn't very well toss her over his shoulder and bundle her into the coach.

She reminded him of a cornered deer—ready to bound away at the smallest provocation.

"Fletcher lets lodgings above the common rooms. I'm sure he'd provide us each with a chamber." Leonidas slid a glance to his coach.

Excellent.

Baldwin and Farrel had returned and begun securing his belongings.

A grin played around the corners of his mouth when he considered Shenton-Wayford's reaction when the whey-faced reprobate awoke in the middle of the Atlantic. It was better than the buggering ponce deserved.

"I haven't funds to pay for lodgings." Humiliation rendered Miss McKessick's words formal and stiff, but the proud tilt of her chin and squared shoulders belied defeat.

"Have you any serving experience?" Leonidas asked. "My brother is always looking for reliable help."

Her face brightened, and she managed a budding smile. "Yes. I worked in my father's... That is, since I was a young child, I've worked in a tavern and inn. I can cook, serve, clean, keep the books, order supplies. Oversee employees. Just about anything that needs doing."

"Perfect." Leonidas took her bags and headed toward the coach.

After a moment's hesitation, she fell into step beside him.

"Do you want to walk, or would you prefer to ride in the coach?" he asked.

After her earlier experience, he could well understand

her reluctance to enter a conveyance with a man she didn't know.

A few fat raindrops plopped onto them.

"In truth, sir, I'm fairly exhausted. I've been up since three this morning and don't relish walking the streets in the rain."

Neither did Leonidas, especially as evening descended, and they'd have to traverse a few less desirable neighborhoods before reaching *De la Chance.*

"The coach it is, then." He offered an encouraging smile. "By the by, I'm Leonidas Westbrook."

Her expression changed not a jot.

How refreshing to come upon someone who didn't know the Westbrook name. He'd deliberately not added *Lord* before his name as was proper because the truth of it was, in his experience, the title *Lord* or *Lady* seldom reflected a person's true character. Evidently, she hadn't heard Baldwin address him as *my lord* either.

"As you've no doubt concluded, I am Primrose McKessick. I appreciate your assistance." She bit her full lower lip again. "But I fear you'll miss the tide, Mr. Westbrook."

He shrugged, not nearly as put upon as he ought to have been by the situation. "As to that, I think it better all-around if Shenton-Wayford takes my cabin. His absence for at least three months should serve you well. I'll book passage on the next ship sailing to Greece."

"He'll be utterly furious." She chuckled, a low throaty purr, and Leonidas felt something peculiar unfurling behind his ribs. "But I applaud your boldness. I wish I could see his expression when he awakens."

"As would I." Leonidas handed her into the vehicle and placed her valises beside her. "Give me a few minutes to speak with my drivers."

Nodding, she rested her head against the luxurious squabs, and her eyelids fluttered closed.

After informing Baldwin and Farrel of his decision to impose upon Fletcher, he hopped inside the coach only to find Miss McKessick sound asleep.

"You are far too trusting, Miss McKessick," he murmured as he settled onto the opposite bench.

"Not *that* trusting, Mr. Westbrook."

A cunning smile arched her pretty bowed mouth, and as she opened her eyes, she slowly withdrew a small, evil-looking dirk from beneath her thigh. "And lest you believe I don't know how to use this blade, I assure you I'm quite adept."

He cocked an eyebrow, half in amusement and half in sardonic disbelief. "You would have me believe you've defended yourself with *that*."

He flicked his fingers toward the knife.

Tilting her head, she met his gaze, a challenge in her hazel-blue depths.

She was no timid, mousy female, to be certain.

In that, she reminded him of his sister too.

"I've drawn blood defending my honor against over-amorous patrons more times than I can count." She dropped her attention to his groin, a wicked smile arching her mouth. "And I nearly unmanned another who ignored my refusal."

Good God.

Just who had Leonidas rescued?

An answering grin swept his mouth upward.

Fletcher would have his hands full with her, and Leonidas would be there to watch. It almost made forgoing his voyage worthwhile.

FIVE

De la Chance – Social Club
London

AN HOUR LATER

S tanding uncertainly in *De la Chance's* extravagant entrance, Primrose couldn't help but crane her neck and gawk. Decorated in black and gold with royal blue accents, the interior bespoke understated elegance and taste. She'd never seen anything so impressive or expensive in her entire life.

The grandeur made her feel insignificant and gauche.

Had Mama been accustomed to this extravagance before life had dealt her an unfair blow? How awful it must've been for her to clean tosspots, vomit from drunken guests, and the myriad of other unpleasant tasks required of an innkeeper's wife.

This luxurious establishment was as different as East was from West compared to Lyster McKessick's rundown hostelry. The place would've crumbled into ruin years ago if it hadn't been for hers and Mama's hard work and economizing.

Stationed on either side of the door, four fierce-looking men wearing identical jet-black suits swept the interior constantly with keen gazes, like well-trained deerhounds. Another pair stood as stern-faced sentinels along a corridor leading to a flight of stairs.

Primrose spotted at least two more lingering just inside a room leading from the entry.

She'd bet her last coin that others were posted throughout the club too.

Just who was Leonidas Westbrook's brother that he required so many guards?

She slid her rescuer a sideways glance.

Who was *he*, for that matter?

Though he had behaved the perfect gentleman, she couldn't permit herself to trust Leonidas Westbrook. In truth, she hadn't ever met a man she could trust completely.

At the docks, Mr. Westbrook's larger coachman, the behemoth with fists the size of small watermelons, had addressed him as *my lord*.

Too preoccupied with her situation and reeling from shock at nearly having been prostituted, she'd set that tidbit aside in a corner of her mind.

Now, she drew it forth.

Was it simply a deferential courtesy, or was Mr. Westbrook aristocracy?

Probably the latter, given the luxurious equipage's crest and his expensive togs.

The vehicle was so well sprung and the benches and squabs so lavish, she'd nearly dozed off thrice on the way here. A very dangerous lapse, indeed.

Mr. Westbrook had seemed content to travel in silence, for which she was grateful.

Her jumbled thoughts required sorting.

A maelstrom of emotions had pummeled her since Mr. Westbrook had exposed Chesley's nefarious scheme. Even now, Primrose's stomach quivered, and had she been a weaker woman, she might've cast up her accounts. Except there wasn't much to vomit as she hadn't eaten since her simple breakfast of tea and toast because that's all she could afford.

A trio of pretty women in matching elegant but modest black gowns, their heads together as they spoke, passed by the opening. *Scottish Terriers.* Assuredly not the attire one would expect of ladies of the evening, not that Primrose had much knowledge of such things.

At home, gossip had it that Widow Begbie made her

favors available for the right price, and an unremarkable cottage on Dingwall's outskirts was rumored to be a house of ill repute. From time to time, Primrose had seen the four women who lived there. All appeared tired, disillusioned, and aged beyond their years.

Rather than judge them, for surely their profession wasn't by choice, she pitied them.

Perhaps there hadn't been anyone to rescue them from that undesirable trade.

A woman without resources had few options.

"Leonidas! I could scarcely take it in when Brindlecombe informed me you were here."

A man with wavy chestnut-colored hair and bottle-green eyes strode down the corridor and into the foyer. The bespectacled man Mr. Westbrook had greeted when he and Primrose arrived, and who'd trotted off to find his employed, accompanied him.

Gorden Setter, she mentally noted, taking in Mr. Westbrook's brother.

She really must stop comparing people to dogs.

After the little man resumed his place behind the elegant rosewood counter and adjusted his spectacles, he began sorting through stacks of receipts. Now and again, he tutted or *tisked* to himself.

Attired entirely in black except for his gold and black paisley waistcoat and gold neckcloth glinting with a sapphire pin, Mr. Westbrook's brother's height, angular cheeks, and full mouth hinted at his relation to her rescuer.

"I thought you sailed this eve." Expression inquisitive, he embraced her champion. "Was I mistaken?"

His verdant gaze probed Primrose for a disconcerting moment before he returned his attention to Leonidas Westbrook.

"As to that..." Leonidas shrugged. "There's been an unforeseen, uncontrollable change in plans, Fletcher."

"Is aught amiss?" Fletcher Westbrook must have silently signaled his henchmen because they drew nearer, one hand braced on the pistols shoved into their trousers' waistbands.

An involuntary shudder rippled up Primrose's spine.

Had she jumped from the proverbial frying pan into the fire?

Did she truly wish to work here?

Trepidation and hesitation trailed dual paths across her shoulders.

What choice had she?

Go back to Dingwall, Scotland?

Take her chances on London's streets where the likes of Chesley and Hadleigh roamed?

No, thank you.

Far better to stay right here and pray she didn't come to regret it.

"Of course, something *is* wrong." The proprietor

twisted his lips into a wry grin. "You wouldn't be here if it weren't."

Again, he skimmed that disturbing gaze over Primrose.

Did he believe Primrose posed him or his brother a threat?

She almost laughed out loud.

What could she possibly do with a half dozen, likely highly trained and dangerous, armed henchmen lurking nearby and likely a dozen more prowling the establishment?

Besides, the club owner towered over her by at least a foot.

Nevertheless, she *could* wield the dirk Mama had purchased and insisted Primrose learn to use to protect herself from being set upon and ruined.

Leonidas gestured for Primrose to come forward, which she did with reluctance weighting her scuffed boots. "Fletcher, please allow me to introduce Primrose McKessick. Miss McKessick, my brother, Fletcher Westbrook, the proprietor of this fine establishment."

He bowed, and Primrose managed a passable curtsy. "Sir."

How was she to address him when they were both Mr. Westbrook?

In her thoughts, she could use their first names.

No one would ever know.

"Might we speak in privacy, Fletch?" Leonidas removed his hat, then cupped his nape. "We have a bit of a conundrum."

"Come." Fletcher nodded and slid that far too perceptive gaze toward Primrose again. "Let's adjourn to my office, shall we?"

Primrose made to fetch her valises, but he held up a hand. "No need, Miss McKessick. My men shall see they are undisturbed."

Even as he spoke, a monstrous bald fellow gathered them in one hand as if they weighed no more than a loaf of bread and disappeared into another room with a gold placard on the door marked "*Private.*"

"Refreshments?" Fletcher directed the question to her.

Primrose had opened her mouth to decline when her dratted stomach chose to growl with the intensity of a starved lion. Mortification made her cheeks burn like hot coals.

Two of the dangerous-looking fellows exchanged a humor-filled glance.

"Yes. I do believe refreshments are in order." Fletcher lifted his chin. "Chandler. See to it and please deliver them yourself."

"Aye, boss." A wiry fellow with a scar on his forehead paralleling his right eyebrow nodded and slipped away on eerily silent feet.

Yorkshire terrier.

Stop it, Primrose.

Leonidas leaned down and murmured into her ear. "Morrey Chandler is Fletcher's second in command and head of security."

Five minutes later, Primrose sat in a delightfully comfortable royal blue armchair before an enormous rosewood desk.

Though thoroughly masculine and matching the decorative theme of the rest of the club, from the black and blue Aubusson carpet to the gold brocade sofas, the room also held welcoming touches.

Blue and gold tasseled throw pillows on the sofa; yellow roses in a Campana Spode vase atop the Italian black marble fireplace mantel, flanked on either side by gilt and crystal drop candlesticks; elaborately cut decanters atop what must surely be a mahogany liquor cabinet, which also displayed a black and gold bone china tea set.

One hip resting on his brother's desk as if it were habit, Leonidas spun his hat in circles with his long fingers.

Arms folded, Fletcher leaned a shoulder against a full bookcase and, without a qualm or adherence to decorum, regarded her. Literally, like a hawk watching its prey before it swooped in and seized the unsuspecting creature with its sharp talons and flew away to feast.

Really.

Must he be so suspicious?

Clearing her throat, Primrose uncrossed her ankles and clasped her hands in her lap atop her serviceable slate-colored gown. She hadn't any other options. But Lord help her, if she had, she would have dashed from the room in a trice.

These Westbrook men were wholly unnerving.

"The thing is, Fletcher, I've just rescued Miss McKessick from an abduction attempt by the West End Whoremaster."

SIX

Primrose's stomach plunged to her feet again. She'd come so very close to ruination.

Leonidas tossed his hat on his brother's tidy desk. It landed near an ormolu and brass pen stand. He proceeded to remove his black leather gloves.

Primrose didn't own a pair of gloves and sudden shame at her work-roughened hands and short nails made her tuck her fingers under her thighs.

"Her cousin had arranged to sell her to Hadleigh, Fletch."

Undeniable anger sharpened Leonidas's noble features.

Fletcher's eyebrows crashed together, and fury sparked in his eyes.

"Bloody sodding ponce," he said tightly.

Primrose knew Chesley was a rotter, but she never imagined he'd stoop so low. His financial circumstances must be dire, but that was not her fault and wasn't an excuse for his reprehensible behavior.

"Torrian came upon us at the docks. He's investigating Hadleigh." Leonidas sent Primrose an apologetic glance from beneath his thick eyelashes.

He did have the most lovely blue eyes.

Primrose might get lost in them if she permitted herself the luxury.

Which, of course, she absolutely would not.

Leonidas rubbed his nose as if he were reluctant to continue. "Seems several, ah, ladybirds, have turned up dead under mysterious circumstances."

Primrose's heart stalled for a moment, and she stifled a gasp.

Sweet Lord.

She hadn't heard that exchange.

Assuredly, the *ladybirds* he referred to were not the cute red and black beetles she let climb up her fingers as a child. She couldn't prevent the humiliating flush sailing up her cheeks or renewed relief that Leonidas Westbrook had rescued her.

His alertness and consideration, as well as his sacrifice, had saved her from unspeakable horror.

Fletcher whistled.

"By God, Hadleigh's become brazen. And you say her cousin was involved?" He shook his dark head. "I'm deeply sorry you had to experience such horror, Miss McKessick."

"Thank you, sir."

For now, she'd decided to address him as sir and Leonidas as Mr. Westbrook.

Leonidas stood just as someone rapped on the door.

"Yes?" Fletcher took a defensive stance.

The man was certainly on the alert, which begged the question: why?

"It's Chandler, sir, with the refreshments."

"Come in, Chandler."

Chandler entered and set a laden tray on a low tea table before the sofas. "Is there anything else, sir?"

"No, thank you." Fletcher shook his head. "Have the men start their rounds early tonight and more frequently. Every ten minutes."

"Yes, sir." Chandler didn't appear the least troubled about his employer's odd request.

Once his man had left, Fletcher motioned for Primrose to come to the sofas.

"Come, Miss McKessick. You can eat while we discuss

why my brother brought you here." A twinkle entered his eyes. "Though I think I can guess."

Leonidas grinned and extended a hand to help Primrose.

She couldn't fault them for their manners.

As she laid her fingers in his hand, she noticed several ink stains on his fingers. He smelled good too. She'd first noticed his cologne in the coach. Not sweet or overpowering but musky and slightly woodsy. Cedar or eucalyptus, perhaps.

"We shall require rooms, Fletch."

Leonidas released her hand and followed her to the sofas, where he folded his tall frame onto a cushion with masculine grace. Without hesitation, he piled the china plate with an assortment of tasty sandwiches, cold meats, cheese, and fruit. "She also needs a position and has extensive experience."

"Of course, you shall have rooms." Fletcher waved a well-manicured hand as if his brother were foolish even to ask. After joining Leonidas on the sofa and helping himself to a ham sandwich, he leaned back and crossed his legs.

"Tell me about your experience, please, Miss McKessick."

In the process of taking a sip of rather good lemonade, Primrose nodded as she swallowed and set the glass aside. As briefly as possible and without revealing names or locations, she explained how she'd worked in the hostelry since childhood.

"I kept the accounts for the past seven years. Tended to the banking and inventory. I also ordered the supplies. Oh, and I'm educated and well-schooled in decorum. My mother was the daughter of a viscount. I read, speak, and write French fluently, and I also speak Italian and a smattering of Spanish."

No need to include that she'd nursed her mother and brother.

Those skills weren't pertinent to this position—whatever it was.

An unreadable glance passed between the brothers.

Other than with Mama, who tried to shield her from the unpleasantness that was Lyster McKessick, Primrose had never shared that kind of intimacy with anyone.

Not even Oleander.

He'd always been too sickly.

Fletcher leaned forward, his elbows on his knees, and steepled his fingers. He stared at her with such focused intensity Primrose almost squirmed upon her cushion. After several nerve-racking moments in which she tried to consider what she'd do if he refused to hire her, he tilted his strong chin, evidently having come to a decision.

He rose, collected a black leatherbound ledger off his desk, and handed it to her. "There seem to be discrepancies recorded here. Will you take a look and tell me your thoughts?"

"Certainly." Primrose set her plate aside, surprised she'd been able to eat a bite under the circumstances. After folding her serviette—gold and monogrammed with *DLC* —she accepted the bookkeeping journal.

Her stomach a bundle of capering nerves, she opened the ledger, then flipped to the last page. She studied the entries for a few moments to understand the system. Then she started with the final entry and worked backward, mentally making notes.

After a few minutes, she gave a cautious nod.

He was correct.

There were suspicious entries.

Very subtly and cleverly done too.

In her opinion, someone stole from Fletcher, but she suspected he already knew that. Acute intelligence shone in his eyes—Leonidas's too, for that matter.

Who were these Westbrooks?

She raised her gaze and met his eyes. "I would need to see the invoices, bills of sale, and receipts to be certain, but there are inconsistencies and even double entries."

Shifting her attention to Leonidas Westbrook for a moment, she found him regarding her with interest. He gave her an encouraging smile. "Go on."

He truly was a decent man.

Primrose pointed at a line.

"See this, sir? The amount is identical to this entry for the same vendor." She flipped back two pages and indicated another entry. "One is for brandy, but the other is for whisky."

She glanced upward. "I'd guess both products are on the same bill of sale."

"Yes, I perceived that as well." Fletcher's tone revealed nothing.

Leonidas whistled, then winked at her. "Well done, Miss McKessick."

Naturally, the flush rushing to her hairline wasn't because he was so deuced charming. It was relief-born. That was all.

Quirking an eyebrow, Fletcher brushed a hand over his jaw.

"I'd originally thought to give you a position serving tables, but I believe, Miss McKessick, *De la Chance* would fare better with you keeping the books. My current bookkeeper is about to receive his *congé*."

And rightly so, if he'd been cheating his employer.

"I have to admit, I never cared for Mercer Nisbet, Fletcher." Leonidas stretched his legs out. "Always thought he was too much of a sycophant, bookkeeper or not."

"Duly noted," Fletcher said dryly before giving Primrose an easy smile. "That is if you're interested in the position. I know it's not what you expected, and no doubt eyebrows will be raised. However, I've never cared overly much about perceived propriety. The pay is three guineas monthly for the first six months and five thereafter. Plus quarterly bonuses. I shall also provide you with a suitable wardrobe. Room and board are included. What say you?"

He extended his hand.

"Yes. *Yes.* Please." Relief, excitement, and anticipation thrummed through Primrose. She rose swiftly, bumping her knee on the table, and the tray rattled, sending the sandwiches bouncing.

She shook his hand, still in a state of awe.

He hadn't asked for references or where she'd gained her experience. The fewer people that knew she'd fled an arranged marriage in Scotland, the better.

"Excellent." Fletcher rubbed his palms together. "I've interviewed four other experienced bookkeepers, and none found the inconsistencies you did, Miss McKessick."

Primrose marshaled her courage. "Sir?"

"Yes?" He turned from his desk where he'd placed the ledger.

"It might be rather confusing if I address you and your brother as Mr. Westbrook. Do you have another preference?" She slid her regard to Leonidas. "Or do you?"

Grinning like a Cheshire cat with a bowl of fresh cream, Fletcher folded his arms and shot his brother a teasing look.

"Don't." Glowering, Leonidas shook his midnight head.

Fletcher ignored his obvious discouragement. "So my wayward half-brother neglected to tell you he's a duke's son, did he? May I present Lord Leonidas Westbrook, the third biological son of my adopted father, the Duke of Latham? You may call him Lord Leonidas."

A duke's son?

But he hadn't wanted Primrose to know.

Why?

SEVEN

De la Chance Private Dining Room

A FORTNIGHT LATER – MORNING

As he had every morning since showing up at Fletcher's doorstep two weeks ago, Leonidas joined his brother and the other selected staff from his three enterprises to discuss today's agenda.

Fletcher was nothing if not highly organized. He expected much from his employees—loyalty above all else —but he also treated his staff extremely well.

Leonidas surveyed the assembled men and women— quite an eclectic troupe, but they worked well together. He'd spent considerable time with Fletcher these past several months and had come to know and admire his employees.

Morry Chandler chatted with Fred Brindlecombe, the concierge, and Mrs. Bernicia Dough, the lead cook. Ellora Rudgate, the serving and social staff supervisor, listened to something Dawson Clemmons, Fletcher's secretary, said.

Armand Chambeau—in charge of club entertainment and managing Fletcher's theater—slathered berry preserves on a crumpet. Lastly, Primrose, the bookkeeper, the newest and youngest member of the select group, watched them all from beneath a fringe of gold-tipped eyelashes.

He'd observed that about her.

She didn't say much but took in everything. Likely, she was still feeling a mite uncertain in her new surroundings but seemed to be adjusting well enough.

Fletcher had wasted no time dismissing his former bookkeeper, Mercer Nisbet.

The devious jackanape was lucky Fletcher hadn't brought the belligerent and unremorseful thief up on charges. But then, Fletcher always had been too compassionate, which was why he'd gone into medicine and then abruptly given it up over a decade ago.

He didn't speak of that time, nor had he revealed why he'd left the profession.

Leonidas slid into the only vacant seat, which, happily, was next to Primrose.

She sent him a half-smile before lifting her teacup to her pink mouth.

No longer did she wear her worry around her like a thick cloak.

According to Fletcher, she'd stepped into her new role with exceptional professionalism and skill. The other employees still exercised caution regarding her. But that was to be expected, even though the threat to them, the clubs, and Fletcher no longer existed. Everyone had been on edge for so long that it would take time for them to accept they no longer needed to be on guard all the time.

For over a year, someone had targeted Fletcher's clubs; after two death threats and numerous vandalisms, he'd left London so Torrian could investigate on his behalf. A couple months ago, Torrian caught the culprit. Since then, nothing untoward had occurred.

"Please excuse my tardiness." Leonidas unfolded his serviette and laid it across his lap. "I paid a visit to the docks early this morning."

A footman placed an overfull plate before him and then poured his tea.

"Thank you, Humphrey." Leonidas smiled at the newly hired fellow trying hard to impress Fletcher. If he performed his duties well, he'd eventually move to serving the club's prestigious guests.

"Any luck?" Fletcher plunked two sugar lumps into his coffee before stirring the black-as-pitch liquid.

Leonidas suppressed a shudder.

How his brother could drink that stuff was beyond him.

Leonidas had tasted the finest coffee Turkey, Brazil, and Spain had to offer, and that swill Fletcher drank every morning was an insult to coffee beans.

Cutting a bite of sausage, Leonidas shook his head. "Not yet, but I knew it would be several weeks before another ship sailed to Greece."

"I'm sorry to have been an inconvenience, Lord Leonidas." Primrose spoke so softly that Leonidas barely heard her. "But I'm not sorry Chesley is sailing across the ocean, or that I have a new position. I owe you much, and I am grateful."

The smile she bestowed upon Leonidas momentarily blinded him.

His head swam dizzily, and the room suddenly felt stifling hot.

Mayhap he'd caught a bit of the ague.

What other explanation was there for this physical onslaught?

She wore one of the five gowns Fletcher had commissioned for her—a simple, modest affair in dark blue. The shade brought out the azure in her eyes and the flaxen ribbons in her sandy blond tresses she'd twisted into a simple but becoming chignon. The color was quite a concession for Fletcher, who normally required all his employees to wear black.

That begged the question, why?

Was Fletcher, an admitted rogue, interested in Primrose other than professionally?

Leonidas's stomach pitched, and it wasn't because the sausage was bad or he'd caught a chill.

Fletcher never became involved with an employee.

Never.

It was one of his self-imposed rules.

Regardless, that didn't mean Leonidas's half-brother didn't know his way around a lady's boudoir. Women adored him, and Fletcher was a confessed rake. But Primrose McKessick was unlike any woman Leonidas had ever met, and perchance, Fletcher found her every bit as fascinating.

I do not find her fascinating.

I merely admire her stalwartness.

Cutting her a sidelong glance, Leonidas again experienced that foreign flicker behind his ribs. Mayhap there was something wrong with his heart.

Yes. Yes. That must be it.

Perhaps he'd ask Fletcher to examine him.

Keep trying to convince yourself of that, Leonidas Rafe Desmond Westbrook.

You might come to believe it.

Leonidas couldn't identify the nasty feeling rooting around his belly—it assuredly was *not* jealousy—but it put him off his food.

He pushed his plate away and took up his teacup.

It made no difference to him if Fletcher had taken a romantic interest in Primrose. As soon as he could book passage, Leonidas meant to leave the country—perhaps for years.

He had a book to write.

His previous travels had lasted more than four years.

Who knew how long he'd be gone this time?

"Aren't you hungry this morning?" Crinkling her upturned nose, Primrose looked between him and his plate.

Not anymore.

"Miss McKessick?" Mrs. Dough, her triple chins folding like a hefty fan, leaned forward. "I have the supply and inventory lists you requested. Shall we go over them this morning?"

Primrose glanced at Fletcher for confirmation, and he nodded. "Yes. Shall we say at half ten?"

A commotion in the corridor drew Leonidas's attention to the closed door. It burst open, and Cassius and Darius piled in, arms around the other's shoulders.

"Surprise!" they cried in unison.

Cassius puzzled his forehead when his attention landed on Leonidas.

"Leonidas? What are you doing here?"

"It's a long story," Fletcher offered dryly.

"Not that long," Leonidas challenged.

"Twins?" Primrose whispered beside Leonidas. "Good heavens, how does one tell them apart?"

He leaned close to whisper in her ear. A foolish endeavor when her sweet essence wafted past his nose, and the little mole on her silky earlobe proved quite the most tempting speck.

Get a hold of yourself, man.

Bloody good thing he would be aboard a ship soon.

Miss Primrose McKessick was a distraction Leonidas neither wanted nor needed.

Straightening, he tossed his serviette on the table. "Truthfully, we often couldn't when they were young. The scamps would trade places and fool us all."

He stood, and Fletcher followed suit.

"Those are more of the Westbrook brothers," Miss Rudgate, rail-thin, prune-faced, but a genius at organizing, informed a bewildered Primrose beneath her breath while the brothers embraced.

"How many are there?" Primrose asked in a hushed tone.

"Seven, counting the two older adopted sons," Miss Rudgate explained with a haughty air of self-importance. "Our employer is one of the adopted. There's a daughter too. She's the youngest."

"Eight?" Primrose's voice held a note of awe. "How wondrous."

Leonidas couldn't prevent the indulgent smile he

sent her.

"Have you eaten?" Fletcher asked the twins after the brothers had hugged one another.

"Not yet." Cassius shook his head, glancing around the full table. "I'm famished."

"I'm finished. You may have my seat." Mr. Chambeau pushed his chair back with his usual dramatic flair. The Frenchman enjoyed an audience. "If there is nothing else, Mr. Westbrook, I shall be off. *Zut,* there is so much to do."

"I'll stop by the theater this afternoon, Armand." Fletcher shook his hand and then turned to the twins. "Sit down. Eat."

The other employees also excused themselves, including Primrose. She brushed crumbs off her gown. "Please excuse me."

"Does this mean you are a civilian once again?" Leonidas clapped Darius on the shoulder and eyed his buff trousers and whisky-brown coat. "I thought you had a few months remaining."

"It does indeed, brother. My commanding officer was willing to apply my unused leaves of absence to ensure his newly commissioned nephew would take my position." Darius's unabashed grin declared how delighted he was. "Now I have to figure out what to do with the rest of my life. Opening a bookstore still holds possibilities. Perhaps a bookstore and coffee shoppe."

A sweet smile curving her mouth, Primrose followed the others from the room.

Leonidas refused to watch her leave—or rather denied himself the pleasure of watching her gently swaying hips.

This momentary fascination with Primrose McKessick would fade.

It must.

"She's new." Cassius plopped into her chair and plucked toast from Leonidas's plate. Happily munching on the triangle, he spoke with his mouth full. "Pretty little thing. Did I detect the merest Scots accent?"

Leonidas nodded.

"*She* is why our dear brother is not aboard a ship sailing to Greece at this very moment. He's become a rescuer of damsels in distress." Fletcher resumed his seat and took up his now cold coffee. "She's also my new, very competent bookkeeper."

"I'm positive there's a fascinating tale buried there somewhere." Cassius waggled his eyebrows.

Darius also sat but turned and stared at Primrose's retreating form. Furrows etched twin lines across his forehead. He tapped the back of the chair with his fingertips. "A fellow on the docks yesterday and today asked if anyone had seen a Scottish lass matching her description."

Bloody, sodding...

Clenching his jaw, Leonidas met Fletcher's potent scrutiny.

His tense expression said he'd jumped to the same troubling conclusion.

"Bulldog of a man? Muscular? Squat?" Leonidas gripped the back of his chair.

"No." Darius shook his head. "This chap had the look of a detective or an investigator. Tidy suit. Scuffed boots. Quite thorough. Knew his stuff. Even had a sketch of the woman."

A knot formed in Leonidas's stomach.

That information could not portend anything good.

Darius pointed to the now empty doorway. "I'll re-enlist if that young woman is not who he's trying to find, and I promise you, my days in His Majesty's Navy are over."

"Did he say why he sought her?" His mind racing for an explanation, Leonidas slid onto his chair.

There might be innumerable reasons.

Primrose had said she'd escaped—*something*.

"No." Darius offered Humphrey a grateful smile before spearing a steaming sausage with his fork. "Which I take to mean he doesn't want people to know his purpose. Had she been a criminal, wouldn't he have tried to warn people?"

He had a valid point.

That didn't mean Primrose wasn't a fugitive, however.

Many a pretty face concealed a wicked heart.

That notion made Leonidas quite ill.

Though nothing about Primrose alluded to treachery or dishonesty.

Cassius scratched his temple before meeting Fletcher's and Leonidas's gazes in turn. "What, exactly, do you know about your new bookkeeper?"

"Not as much as I ought to, it seems." Fletcher leaned back and, after giving Leonidas a long look, pulled his earlobe. "I think another discussion with Miss McKessick is in order. Let's also contact Torrian and put him on the investigator's tail. That could prove quite useful."

"Excellent suggestion." Leonidas nodded, but his thoughts were elsewhere.

Why was an investigator looking for Primrose?

What hadn't she told Leonidas?

Of most importance, precisely what had she escaped from?

EIGHT

De la Chance
Outside Fletcher Westbrook's Office

FOUR HOURS LATER

Standing before Fletcher's walnut-paneled office door, Primrose drew in a lungful of air while commanding her cavorting pulse to steady.

The summons wasn't unexpected.

In truth, she'd been waiting for it all morning. She'd overheard one of the twin's remarks about a man searching for a Scottish lass that matched her description.

She'd nearly cast up her breakfast right there on the expensive carpet.

Her stomach plummeted to her new shoes, and she vowed her heart had stopped beating for at least three *tick-tocks* of the stately veneered walnut longcase clock in the corridor as she raced with her hand over her mouth across the Aubusson runner to her chamber.

Not a cold, fusty attic corner smelling of stale ale, old cabbage, and onions that she shared with mice and spiders as had been her assigned resting place in Dingwall. But an actual chamber with a rosewood four-poster bed, dressing table, armoire, and coal fireplace framed by an ornately carved oak mantel.

For the first time in her life, she slept in a warm room, upon a real mattress, covered herself with a decadent embroidered gold and cobalt blue counterpane, washed at a lovely blue and white porcelain tiled washstand, and even bathed in a copper tub with scented soap.

Arms clutched around her middle for that first torturous half hour, Primrose had paced back and forth across her chamber's plush carpet, battling panic and the urge to pack her belongings and flee.

Where too?

She had no money. No friends or family.

Outside, a springtime storm raged.

It was nothing compared to the tempest howling within her.

Later, during her meeting with Mrs. Dough, Primrose

could scarcely concentrate on the woman's words. She'd asked the cook to leave the inventory records, promising to return them this afternoon, along with a list of supplies Primrose would order.

If she were here this afternoon.

God above, she could hardly breathe for worry.

In truth, with the two and twenty armed guards Fletcher Westbrook employed, she couldn't be any place safer than *De la Chance*.

Not a single doubt assailed her that Wallace MacLerie had hired the detective.

Lyster would have never parted with the coin to do so.

How had the baron found her so quickly?

Besides using a fake name, she'd left false trails on every leg of her journey to London.

She'd been so careful.

Pressing her lips together, she gave the slightest shake of her head.

Obviously, not careful enough.

If Primrose had been aboard the *Sea Queen*, MacLerie mightn't ever have located her. Now, however, she entertained very real fear that he would.

Had he journeyed to London to retrieve her?

Or had he only hired someone to find her?

She just needed two more weeks.

On May thirtieth, she would be of age.

Then it wouldn't matter what arrangement Lyster had made. No one could force her to wed the baron. Honestly, she wasn't positive Lyster and MacLerie's agreement was legal.

Primrose smoothed her palms down the front of her gown, quite the nicest she'd ever owned, before assuring her chignon remained tidy. If she were about to be dismissed, she'd do so with dignity and poise.

And she would not cry.

At least not until she'd reached her bedchamber.

The Westbrooks had treated her kindly and deserved to know the truth. She'd never intended to be deceptive, but by omission, she had been.

She rapped once upon the door.

"Come."

Marshaling every ounce of her fortitude, she pressed the shiny brass handle and entered.

Leonidas stood with his back to the fire crackling happily in the hearth.

He bent his mouth into a brief but gentle smile.

She searched the room.

He was alone.

Where was Fletcher?

Her pulse accelerated, and a wave of nausea buffeted her.

Had Fletcher asked Leonidas to discharge her because

he'd been the one to bring her to *De la Chance* in the first place?

"Please close the door, Primrose, and have a seat." He indicated the sofa rather than the chairs before the desk. "Fletcher felt you might be more comfortable speaking with me."

Her unease abated a trifle.

So this wasn't to be an official interrogation?

A swell of relief engulfed her.

That was a good sign.

Wasn't it?

After doing as he bid and arranging her skirts, Primrose folded her hands in her lap.

He perched on the sofa's arm and regarded her with those unfathomable indigo eyes.

"Darius shared troublesome news with us this morning."

She might as well be forthright. Pretending she didn't know what Leonidas referred to benefited no one. Perhaps in this small way, she might prove her integrity.

"Yes, I overheard." Studying her clasped fingers, she swallowed. Forcing herself to meet Leonidas's understanding gaze, she said, "I told you I escaped. What I didn't tell you was why. It's not a pretty tale, I fear, but I assure you, I am not a criminal."

The merry fire sizzled and popped as if everything

were right in the world while rain furiously pelted the window as if punishing the glass.

Wasn't that just like life?

Everything seemed a juxtaposition.

Leonidas shifted until he sat beside her, their knees mere inches apart.

She'd greatly inconvenienced him, yet he'd never blamed her or complained.

He was particularly handsome today in a cobalt jacket trimmed in black velvet that did enchanting things to his eyes and made his midnight-black hair glisten.

"Why don't you tell me about it," he urged in that melodic baritone that sent shivers down her arms. "I promise you can trust me."

Could she?

How Primrose wanted to.

And why was he being so nice?

It made her feel all that much more guilty.

As succinctly as possible, she explained her birth, Mama's and Oleander's deaths, Lyster's ongoing hatred and abuse, and his arranging a marriage for her against her will.

"I shall not marry Wallace MacLerie, baron or not. In two weeks, I'll be of age. I do not care that Lyster spent the money the baron gave him for me." She fairly shook with her vehemence. "I'm not a cow, horse, or hog to be bought and sold."

A deep chuckle rumbled upward from Leonidas's chest, and merriment danced in his black-lashed eyes.

She gaped, suddenly angry he should find her plight amusing.

"I'm glad my situation humors you, Lord Leonidas," she snapped.

NINE

Still on the Sofa

A DOZEN HEARTBEATS LATER

Embarrassment and irritation heating her blood, Primrose shifted to stand, but Leonidas laid his large palm upon her hand and rubbed his thumb over the sensitive flesh.

It was quite the most delicious sensation.

Yet even as Primrose acknowledged her growing attraction to him, she forced herself to accept the impossibility of anything coming of it.

Their worlds were too far apart.

Besides, he was leaving for far-off places soon.

"I shall pack my belongings," she forced through stiff lips.

"Hush, Primrose."

She adored how her name sounded on his lips. Slightly husky and perhaps...tinged with tenderness?

If wishes were horses, beggars would ride, she sternly reprimanded herself.

Do not do anything as foolish and nitwitted as to even remotely, for one second, entertain any romantic notions about Lord Leonidas Westbrook.

You'll end up with a broken heart.

"Don't get your feathers ruffled, my prim little hen. I wasn't laughing at you but imagining MacLerie's astonishment at finding your dirk pressed against his nether regions."

Primrose couldn't prevent her jaw from sagging before a giggle throttled up her throat. She'd never used the dirk on MacLerie, but that didn't mean she wouldn't. "I rather like that image myself."

Leonidas relaxed against the sofa and crossed one long leg over the other.

"Tell me about the baron, Primrose. Why is he fixated on you?"

She sighed, loathing to dredge up the past and what she'd left behind in Scotland.

However, she had no choice.

"Wallace MacLerie is the feudal Baron of

Glentorquith. He knows noble blood runs in my veins and wants to improve his bloodline. He purchased his barony and is desperate to produce an heir. He's also a two-time widower. His previous wives—also of noble blood—died under mysterious circumstances, and both died childless."

Leonidas made a rough sound in his throat. "That's a convenient coincidence. How did they die?"

"One fell down a flight of stairs, and the other drowned." Primrose shivered, her blood curdling as she recalled the baron's attempts to court her. "MacLerie attempted to woo me for several years, but he didn't stand a chance while Mama was alive. That changed when she passed away a few months ago, and Lyster accepted his bribe."

"*Hmm*, my cousin Torrian might be interested in these details." Leonidas tapped his fingertips on the sofa's arm. "He's the man I spoke with at the docks. The one that took Hadleigh away. He's also an investigator. So is my brother, Lucius."

"You have six brothers and a sister?"

A midnight brow shot upward in askance at her abrupt change of subject.

Surely, Primrose's face glowed as red as the fire's coals, for he no doubt thought she'd been prying. "Miss Rudgate told me at breakfast when the twins arrived."

"I heard her, and yes, I do. I also have too many

cousins to count. My sister, Althelia, recently married. Lucius and Adolphus both wed recently as well. Fletcher, Layton, and I are confirmed bachelors, so that leaves only the twins to trundle down matrimony's path if they so choose."

So Leonidas never intended to marry.

That shouldn't make Primrose sad. Nevertheless, it did.

Truthfully, she wasn't certain she ever would wed either. To be totally at a man's mercy. To have him own her body, mind, and soul. For him to be able to take her children away at will.

What advantage was there to marriage for a woman except, perchance, partial assurance she wouldn't find herself without resources?

Was the trade-off worth it?

It hadn't been for Mama, who had regretted marrying Lyster McKessick every day of her miserable life.

Primrose shrugged off her melancholy musings.

"It must be nice to have a large family," she murmured.

Hers had been a lonely childhood, what little she'd been allowed to enjoy.

"It is, but we have our skirmishes too. Our snowball fights are legendary." Grinning, Leonidas uncrossed his legs and turned toward her. "Would you mind if I asked Torrian to do a bit of sleuthing? He has connections in

Scotland. He might be able to uncover something useful about MacLerie."

Peering through the window, she considered his request. The springtime gale had abated, and a valiant ray or two of sunshine dared to shine through the petulant clouds.

"I suppose that couldn't hurt." Primrose slowly nodded an affirmation as she searched his face's interesting angles and contours.

What was it about him that piqued her interest?

"Does this mean I'm not dismissed?" she asked.

He quirked his mouth up on one side. "That's Fletcher's decision, but I am confident he won't discharge you. You've done nothing wrong. He had an appointment with Armand but said he would speak with us when he returned."

"I suppose I should get back to work then." Primrose made no move to leave, however.

Leonidas's features tightened.

"Primrose, I suggest you not leave *De la Chance* for any reason. If MacLerie's man should happen to trace you here, our men will deter him. I promise you, he won't get inside the premises."

He was right, and although Primrose hadn't had cause to leave the club until now, something inside her rebelled at the gilded prison she now found herself in. But honesty forced her to face the truth. She had no choice. Far better this gilded prison than chancing MacLerie would capture her.

"I truly regret causing you more trouble, Lord Leonidas." Since the day Primrose had met him, she'd been nothing but a thorn in his side.

He gathered her hand and squeezed her fingers, a sympathetic smile framing his face and creasing the corners of his eyes. "First. You haven't been any trouble. I wouldn't have helped you had I not wanted to. Secondly, can you leave off the 'Lord' bit? I detest it."

Interesting.

Most aristocrats gloried in their importance.

She angled her head. "Why?"

"Why, indeed?"

Leonidas released her fingers before scratching his cheek.

"I prefer to make my way in this world. To be known for what I've done and who I am, not for who my father is. Please don't mistake me. My father is an exceptional man. A genuinely decent and honorable man. Still, whenever anyone learns my father is a duke, their behavior toward me inevitably changes."

"I can only agree to do so when we are alone. It wouldn't be seemly to address you by your given name in front of others." She rose, and he stood as well.

"I'll accept that." He brushed a wayward curl behind her ear, and her breath stalled in her lungs.

"Primrose, what would you have done had I not helped you? Why did you trust me?"

"I honestly do not know the answer to either of those questions, Leonidas."

Gazing up into his eyes, something she didn't understand beckoned her. The silvery flecks in his irises glinted with male interest.

Involuntarily, she swayed closer.

His pupils dilated, and his nostrils flared.

"Do you believe in fate, Primrose?"

His voice had grown raspy and devilishly seductive as he lowered his head, inch by provocative inch, until his mouth hovered over hers.

Did he mean to kiss her?

Wouldn't that be the most marvelous thing?

No. Fool, fool, fool.

Primrose should run.

Now.

Her feet refused to budge.

Oh Lord, help me.

She wanted this.

Be careful, her conscience railed. *Leonidas said himself that he is a confirmed bachelor.*

Yes. Yes, he had.

Primrose might crave his kiss, but she wouldn't jeopardize her position.

Nor would she be his plaything—his amusement until he sailed away.

"No. I do not believe in fate, providence, or destiny. Life is what a person makes it." That wasn't entirely true, but Primrose seized the excuse and ducked under his arm. With undignified alacrity that would've mortified Mama, she sped to the door. "Excuse me. I have work to do."

"Run, my little hen."

Leonidas's guffaw followed her into the corridor and echoed in her ears long after she'd closed the door to her office and covered her flaming face with her hands.

Had Leonidas deliberately become the aggressor to frighten her off?

Surely, the hot, salty tears streaming from her eyes were relief. Or fear that MacLerie had found her. Or grief for Mama and Oleander. Or, perchance, all those things.

They definitely were *not* because she was falling in love with Leonidas Westbrook.

TEN

De la Chance
Fletcher's Private Salon

SIX DAYS LATER — LATE EVENING

Neck stiff from making notes in his journal while bending over and studying the various maps spread out upon the table he'd commandeered in Fletcher's private salon, Leonidas rolled his shoulders and yawned.

He mightn't be able to sail yet, but at least he could complete his itinerary.

A glance at the French Empire patinated and gilded bronze mantel clock revealed half midnight. Royal blue dominated this room, from the brocade chairs and sofa to the drawn curtains and Axminster carpet, although ebony and gold accents assured the room's uniformity with the rest of the club.

He ought to go to bed, but a pair of haunting hazel-blue eyes in an oval face framed by silky blond hair kept him from drifting off. Since the day he'd met her almost three weeks ago, Primrose McKessick had confounded and confused him.

The sooner Leonidas boarded a ship, the sooner his life would resume its normal pace and trajectory. As yet, he didn't know when that would be, and his frustration increased daily.

Not sailing on the *Sea Queen* hadn't caused this angst. No, for the first time in recollection, something—*someone*—held almost as much allure as his wanderings had always done. Truth be told, that dawning truth terrified him—tilted his world hat over boot. Compass over sextant.

The intriguing dervish in a petticoat was *not* part of his life plan.

Primrose could not be.

Leonidas had saved her, providing with her employment and a place to live.

Strictly speaking, Fletcher should be credited with the latter two, but he'd acted at Leonidas's behest. That was as much as he was willing to do. And the fact that he had to keep telling himself those facts, to convince himself to stay on his predetermined path, annoyed and exasperated him.

Until these past weeks, he'd always known his own mind.

One pretty little tempting armful had upended his carefully laid plans with nothing more than an innocent question on a dock. Now, it was almost as if he didn't know himself.

A log fell in the grate, sending sparks swirling upward. Eyeing the dying fire, Leonidas decided against adding another. He wouldn't remain much longer.

Elsewhere in the club, guests would enjoy themselves for another hour and a half until closing time. However, his presence went undetected in this private, invitation-only sanctuary on the building's opposite side.

Fletcher typically made a final round to greet his guests at midnight before seeking his bed and trusting his employees to clean and lock up. His well-trained staff did so with admirable efficiency, not just here but also at *Ivories & Aces,* his other gaming club, and at his small playhouse, *The Theater Emporium,* which featured everything from ballet to acrobats, plays to comic operettas, and concerts to pantomimes.

Normally, Leonidas eschewed *De la Chance's* activities and found his mattress earlier in the evening, where he'd spend an hour or so reading—usually a book about traveling. He'd always preferred to retire and rise early, habits which served him well when roving abroad.

Tonight, however, unable to sleep, he'd finally decided

he might as well accomplish something since slumber eluded him again. For the third night in a row, he'd tossed, turned, punched his pillow, and stared morosely at the royal blue canopy above him.

He bloody well knew why too.

After throwing off his bed coverings, he'd swiftly donned trousers, a shirt, and boots. He'd grabbed his satchel containing maps and journals, then stopped in the kitchen and helped himself to a glass of milk and a generous slice of apple pie, the remnants of which lay across the table.

Resting his hand on his chin, he stared morosely into the salon's fire.

It was his own blasted fault he couldn't sleep, and his conscience plagued him for acting like a deuced imbecile with Primrose.

Leonidas had seen that same adoring glint in other women's eyes that she'd turned on him the other day. Always before, their infatuation had cooled his ardor faster than a February dip in the Atlantic. However, when Primrose gazed up at him, trusting, vulnerable, and unpretentious, that powerful sensation that partially unfurled the day he'd met her expanded further.

If Leonidas let them, he suspected those feelings he refused to acknowledge, let alone name, could overpower him and his will.

In truth, it scared the bloody hell out of him.

That was why he'd gone on the offense, though his methods might not have been the noblest. Leonidas had been desperate to make Primrose leave before he acted the besotted fool and kissed her. Because every male instinct and primal, animalistic drive told him he'd be lost once he tasted her sweet lips.

One kiss would never be enough.

Leonidas had no intention of offering Primrose marriage—or any woman for that matter—and all other arrangements would insult her. He might very well find a sharp dirk in the region of *his* bollocks.

His groin contracted at the unpleasant thought.

To assure Primrose's safety, she must remain at *De la Chance*. She could not leave anytime soon, but Leonidas could. Must, in point of fact, before he lost sight of his vision.

Fletcher, like Leonidas, saw no reason to terminate her employment. He agreed to alert Torrian about MacLerie and posted extra sentries outside the club.

For now, all they could do was wait and watch.

One thing was for certain: Primrose kept things interesting.

Yawning again, Leonidas scratched his bristly chin, then raked his hand through his hair.

He had an appointment with the harbor master at half of eight in the morning. If he didn't find any ships scheduled to sail to Greece for a few more weeks, mayhap he'd return to Hefferwickshire House, his father's grand ducal estate in Cumbria, for a week or so.

At least that would put distance between him and Primrose for a time, although he'd already spent a good portion of the past year and a half at Hefferwickshire. Cassius and Darius left for the country three days ago in the ducal coach, and Leonidas wouldn't have an opportunity to see them or the rest of his family for months—or years.

He tapped his fingers on the table.

What in Hades should he do?

ELEVEN

De la Chance's Private Salon

SEVERAL DISCONCERTING HEARTBEATS LATER

The rub of it was that Leonidas didn't bloody well know what to do.

At one time—before a certain delectable Scottish lass disrupted his life—he'd made decisions in a snap. Now, he waffled back and forth like a dingy on a stormy sea.

Tomorrow night, *De la Chance's* monthly country dancing commenced, followed on the last Thursday of the month by a more formal ball.

Leonidas loved to dance and planned to attend for an hour or two. However, earlier today, Fletcher said Miss

Rudgate informed everyone at the morning meeting that two servers had taken to their beds with influenza.

Primrose generously offered to assist for the evening.

Leonidas had been avoiding her, even forgoing the daily meetings, so he'd decided skipping the dance was the wisest thing to do.

Cupping his tense nape where pebbles had taken up residence, he rubbed the stiffness, despising his cowardice.

"You're a poltroon, Leonidas Rafe Desmond Westbrook," he muttered.

Yes, he was.

When had he become more worried about the feelings taking root in *his* heart and beginning to sprout than Primrose possibly becoming enamored with him?

He must nip that distraction in the bud before it took over his life and changed the course he'd set for himself all those years ago. The explorer in him knew full well that gallivanting off pell-mell without knowing where one was going or what one might encounter was a recipe for disaster.

An unapologetic wanderer, he wanted to travel until he lost his sight and hearing and couldn't walk.

Nothing could keep him in one place.

Leonidas's blood hummed in his veins with anticipation.

Imagine the magnificent wonders he would see and

experience. The colorful adventures he would write for others to enjoy.

He gave a stern nod.

Yes, he had made the right choice to distance himself from Primrose.

It was best for them both.

Shouldn't he be happy, then? At peace?

He was neither, and that bloody confounded him.

A noise in the corridor made him lift his head.

As if his musings had summoned her, Primrose glided into the salon, wearing a chaste nightrobe fastened to her pert chin, her bare toes peeking at him from beneath the white hem. She carried a candle holder in one hand and a book in the other. Her hair unbound and trailing to her waist, she faltered when she caught sight of him.

"Oh." Eyes wide and startled, she clapped a hand to her chest, flattening the fabric over her bosom.

Leonidas dragged his gaze away from the tempting mounds. He refused to ogle her as Lyster McKessick's patrons had done. She deserved more respect.

"You startled me, Leonidas. I didn't know anyone was here." She lifted the book a couple of inches. "Fletcher said I might help myself to the books in the library."

"Please do." Leonidas waved a hand. "I'm about to leave as it is."

She set her book down on a half table near the door

before, after a slight hesitation, drifting closer, curiosity brightening her eyes. "What are you doing?"

"Finalizing my itinerary." He snapped the soft Italian leather journal closed before wrapping the leather strap around the middle and tying it.

She sidled closer. "Are those maps of where you'll go?"

"They are."

Setting her candle down, she grazed her fingertips over the line he'd drawn. Bending her mouth into a wistful, nascent smile, she bent to inspect the cartography.

"How fascinating. The drawings are so intricate and quite beautiful. I envy you." She glanced upward, her gaze clear and unbeguiling, with no hint of infatuation shimmering in her eyes.

Had he imagined her admiration?

"It must be fascinating." She slanted her head. "Dangerous too, I should think."

"At times." Leonidas rolled up one map and tucked it into his satchel. "That's why I spend so much time planning my travels. I don't like surprises."

Nodding, she straightened and brushed a lock of hair off her cheek. "Have you always wanted to travel the world and to write?"

He rubbed his nose.

She conversed politely as if that moment in Fletcher's study had never happened—as if they sat in his parents' drawing room instead of a dimly lit salon past midnight, and both in a state of dishabille.

There was nothing the least proper about this.

"Travel, yes. Write, no." A reluctant chuckle escaped him. "My last tutor, Mr. Peabody Peeleclerk—"

"Truly? Gads, that's an awful name." Mirth twitched the corners of her mouth as she shook her head, and a cloud of fair hair billowed about her shoulders.

Leonidas clasped his hands behind his back to keep from threading his fingers through the tempting mass.

Was God punishing him for some past sin because even though the Good Book promised a man wouldn't be tempted beyond what he could resist, he was within a hair's breadth of succumbing?

"Poor man," she said, hilarity coloring her voice. "What could his parents have been thinking?"

"My brothers and I called him Mr. Pee Pee." Chuckling, Leonidas winked. "*He* didn't appreciate our humor."

She giggled, a musical tinkle that filled his heart with joy. "Aye. That was truly bad of you."

"Peabody despaired that I'd ever pen anything coherent." Leonidas rolled up another map and slid it into its holder. "I learned, however, that writing is much like reading. When you find what you are passionate about, each becomes an enjoyable endeavor rather than an unpleasant task."

"That is true." Eyes alight with wonder, she surveyed the salon. "All these books at one's disposal is quite marvelous, is it not? I intend to read every book here."

By library standards, *De la Chance's* wasn't impressive. Still, Fletcher had filled four six-shelf bookcases. Primrose behaved as if this humble library were Hatchards Bookshop, but to someone deprived of the privilege of reading, it must be wondrous, indeed.

She'd love Hatchards with its different stories and shelves upon shelves of books.

"Primrose, if I can persuade Fletcher to allow us a few guards, would you like to visit Hatchards Bookshop?"

The words Leonidas's mouth of their own accord.

Blister and blast!

Once said, he could hardly retract the hair-brained invitation.

What in the blazes was wrong with him?

It was as if he'd become entranced, bewitched. His thoughts, desires, goals, plans, wishes—even his words— were not his to command any longer.

"Oh, I would." Primrose's face lit up, blinding him with radiance. "But do you think it's safe?"

Pity, or perhaps remorse, caused a nasty twinge near his heart that she should have to live in fear.

Rolling up the last map while chastising himself for being a stupid idiot with a tongue that flapped faster and with less contemplation than a chinwag's, Leonidas shrugged.

"There haven't been any more sightings of the mysterious man inquiring about you. Torrian hasn't come up with anything either. Perchance, the fellow has given up or assumed you boarded a ship."

"Then I'd love to. When?" Winding her mass of hair into a golden rope she laid over one shoulder, she canted her head. "I'll have to get permission for time off."

"I'll let you know." Leonidas's anger with himself made his voice gruff and harsher than intended. "We don't want to rush into something dangerous."

"Yes, of course." Taken aback, she blinked at him. "I'll await your convenience."

Primrose clearly didn't think Leonidas intended to keep his word, and he couldn't utter the reassurance she needed to hear. Because the truth was that Leonidas should never have invited her.

Not when he'd determined to stay away from her.

For her sake and his.

It was as if Leonidas's mind and heart were at odds, each waging a fierce battle for dominance, and he had no idea which would emerge victorious. This conflict might very well rip him asunder since he couldn't fathom any way they might come into agreement.

Had Adolphus and Lucius endured this torture?

They'd ended their torment by marrying the sirens that vexed them to Hades and back.

Leonidas didn't have that option.

You could.

No, I cannot.

The battle was very real.

"I'll bid you goodnight then." Despite him behaving like a foul-tempered brute, she offered one of her sweet smiles. "Sleep well."

Not trusting himself to speak for fear he'd blurt something else impractical or harsh, Leonidas grunted.

Primrose's smile faded, and confusion puckered her forehead.

"Leonidas. We don't have to go to the bookstore. I understand you have better things to do."

How quickly she'd pinpointed his reluctance.

It made him feel all the more like an inconsiderate, churlish boor.

Sighing, Leonidas gave in to the overwhelming desire to touch her. Cupping her shoulders, he selfishly grazed the briefest kiss across her forehead—a butterfly's wings of a touch—no more. Summoning his will, integrity, and honor, he firmly pivoted Primrose toward the door.

"Go to bed, Primrose."

She departed without another word.

As Leonidas left the salon, he glanced at the book she'd set aside.

It was one of his.

I'm in a bloody lot of trouble.

TWELVE

THE NEXT MORNING

Arching her stiff back, Primrose set her empty teacup back onto its saucer. After her encounter with Leonidas last night, sleeping proved futile. Tired, wistful, and discontent, she'd risen early and after dressing, gone straight to work. It helped to keep her mind occupied.

A slight chill remained despite a toasty fire popping in the hearth and the sun streaming through the window behind the desk, bathing her in its golden warmth. Or mayhap it wasn't the office but cynicism and distrust turning her heart and spirit frosty.

Would she end up a frigid, bitter spinster, mad at the world for what she'd missed out on? What could never be? What ought to have been? She didn't want to become a sour old tabby, but confusion and disenchantment had become her constant companions since meeting Leonidas.

Was there ever such a perplexing man as Lord Leonidas Westbrook?

He blew hot and cold worse than a fickle debutante at her first ball, and his fluctuations had her at sixes and sevens. Just when Primrose convinced herself he felt nothing for her, and she'd imagined his interest, he did something unexpected like invite her to Hatchards and kiss her forehead.

What, pray tell, was she to make of either of those?

Granted, the soft brushing of his lips on her skin hadn't been a passionate kiss by any stretch of the imagination, but more like a brotherly peck. Nevertheless, the gentle act had been enough to rob her of sleep as she tried, in vain, to decipher the meaning behind his behavior.

Particularly as he'd been disgruntled immediately after asking her if she'd like to visit the bookstore. It didn't take much insight to recognize he regretted the impulse.

Sighing, she took up the pen once more and examined a receipt.

Unlike Lyster McKessick, Fletcher Westbrook only purchased the best for *De la Chance's* patrons and employees. That was unusual. Most employers skimped on employee provisions, but Fletcher had already proven himself unique by hiring her for a position typically held by men.

Primrose was fortunate to have this post and knew it well. And yet, she would've scrubbed floors and emptied slop pots—tasks Lyster regularly assigned to her—if Fletcher had only needed a maid.

"I thought I heard you in here earlier. Howaya?"

His too-big coat hanging loosely on his lean frame, Sean Kenney strode through the open door and availed himself of the small office's only armchair. Slinging one thin leg over the arm, he swung the other back and forth, revealing his boot's worn sole.

As was his wont, his cap covered the upper portion of his face to his raven eyebrows above indigo eyes, and a faded plaid scarf obscured the lower portion.

Primrose had never seen him otherwise.

"Good morning, Sean."

This had become a daily routine since the day after Primrose arrived, and she looked forward to his visits.

Forming a welcoming smile, she set her pen aside and pushed a tin of biscuits across the rosewood desk. Often teased about his small frame by Fletcher's burly guards, the lad adored biscuits. "Mrs. Dough made these soda bread biscuits yesterday."

"God love that woman," he said in his lilting Irish accent. "I just finished goin' to market with her. I thought me mam could barter, but Mrs. Dough's haggling puts Mam's to shame, God rest her soul."

After helping himself to several biscuits and tucking a few in his pockets for later, Sean took a bite and chewed happily.

As always, his azure gaze glinted with a hint of humor and mischief. He narrowed his eyes, no doubt taking in Primrose's haggard features and the purplish shadows beneath her eyes.

"You look tired, Prim."

Sometimes, as he did just now, Sean appeared a decade older than his sixteen years. Maturity shone in his eyes as if he'd seen, heard, and experienced things a lad should never have done, and they had robbed him of his youth and innocence.

"I'm well enough, Sean. Please don't fret about me. I just had a restless night. Probably something I ate."

Primrose hadn't yet made close friends among the female employees. Regardless, she couldn't very well confide in the lad. Not that she'd have been comfortable revealing her frivolous infatuation with Leonidas to anyone.

After all, he was the boss's titled brother.

Sean cocked his head and touched his pointed chin with his forefinger, his nails surprisingly clean and well-tended. "My mam always said that a good laugh and a long sleep are the two best cures for anything."

Despite her doldrums, Primrose chuckled. "More of your endless Irish wisdom?"

"Aye. I didn't think wishing your troubles be as few and far apart as my grandmother's teeth was appropriate." He shoved the scarf down a couple inches, and grinning, took a bite of biscuit with small, square teeth. "First, I never knew my grandmothers, so I have no way of knowing how many teeth they had. And secondly, you didn't say you were troubled, though your expression rivals wilted cabbage."

"Wilted cabbage? Should I be offended?" Shaking her head, Primrose laughed again. "What are you up to today?"

Hired the week prior to Primrose, the lad carried out any number of tasks, including running errands. Primrose supposed it was only natural for the two newest employees, both orphaned, to form an affinity.

He rolled his thin shoulders.

"Unloading supplies. Painting. Carrying baskets for Mrs. Dough in the market. I've just come from the kitchen." He perked up and leaned forward. "And 'cause most people don't pay attention to folks like me, I'm assigned to watching outside for snoopy blokes."

On Primrose's behalf or because Fletcher was cautious by nature?

Sean had been a wealth of information that first week, including how Fletcher had received two death threats.

Dropping his booted feet to the floor, the lad slapped his knees. "I'd best crack on. Don't want the boss peeved at me."

He glanced longingly at the tin.

"Help yourself, Sean. I'm sure your little brother and sister would enjoy them too."

Sean hadn't revealed much about himself besides having two younger siblings.

"Thank you, Prim."

He bent his mouth into a grateful smile as he pocketed several more treats. He reached the door and then swung back to face Primrose. "A gent in fancy togs passed by twice yesterday, but that's not uncommon. Something about him though—he was a mite peculiar. Raised my hackles, it did."

A chill scuttled up Primrose's spine and settled on her shoulders as if someone had walked across her grave.

"Couldn't help but feel he might be casing the place." Sean scratched the back of his hand. "I reported it to Chandler, but he didn't think the fellow was anyone to fret about."

"I'm sure it was nothing," Primrose murmured.

With a little wave, he slipped into the corridor. "Good morning, my lord."

Perfect.

There was only one lord at *De la Chance* this time of day.

A second later, Leonidas poked his head inside.

Naturally, he looked devastatingly handsome in a burgundy jacket, a gold and wine-colored waistcoat, and black breeches. The man could wear sackcloth and women would drool.

Not her, of course.

Nevertheless, her mouth went unaccountably dry.

Tiny lines of fatigue bracketed his eyes, and for some perverse reason, that pleased Primrose.

Perchance musings of her had kept him awake too.

I was no more than he deserved for disturbing her slumber.

"Fletch says if we want to visit Hatchards, morning is the best time because of the dance tonight. He can spare a few men to accompany us for a couple of hours. That is if you'd still like to go."

Why was Leonidas being solicitous this morning when he'd snapped at her last night?

"I told you it wasn't necessary, Leonidas."

"I know. But I did offer, and I was sincere." His demeanor contrite, he leaned a shoulder against the door-jamb and flashed that disarming smile that sent Primrose's tummy and nerves quivering. "Perhaps we can get an ice at Gunter's Tea Shop too."

Primrose had heard of Gunter's famous ices.

The wisest thing for her heart would be to refuse—to distance herself from Leonidas.

So what to do?

Choose wisdom and deny herself the excursion or accept and put aside her self-doubt for a couple of hours?

Primrose hadn't set foot outside the club since arriving, and truthfully, after being cooped up for almost three weeks, the outing sounded divine.

Decision made, she offered a smile of truce as she closed the inkpot and shut the ledger before rising. "Just let me get my cloak and bonnet. I cannot stay too long, however. There are too many preparations for the dance tonight."

"About that." Leonidas straightened and pulled the sleeve of his jacket back into place, the silver quill cuff link at his wrist glinting in the sunlight. "We, that is Fletcher, Chandler, and I, think it best if you are not at the dance tonight after all."

"Why?" Trying to stifle the alarm pulsing through her, Primrose paused in straightening her desk and pinned her attention on him.

His boot heels clacking on the wood floor, Leonidas traveled farther into the room and glanced around in approval. "You've done wonders with this office, Primrose. I've never seen it so tidy and organized."

"You're deflecting, Leonidas. Why can I not help tonight? Fletcher is short-staffed."

"No alarming reason, I assure you, so don't fret. It's merely a precaution. Fletch arranged for *Ivories & Aces's* servers to fill in for the evening." His blue eyes softened, and he touched her shoulder. He seemed unable to resist, just as she could not reprimand him for overreaching.

"The country dances always bring a large crowd and many new guests. Everyone shall be vetted as much as possible, but that doesn't mean someone mightn't slip in. We'd prefer you stayed in your chamber tonight."

As much as she hated to admit it, he was right.

Still, she couldn't resist a pert retort.

"No doubt with an armed guard or three nearby?" A wry smile tugged her mouth upward.

His elevated brow provided the silent confirmation.

Conceding she had no choice, she sighed as she pushed her chair in.

"I'm of age May thirtieth, and then Lyster McKessick no longer has power over me, nor can he speak on my behalf. The agreement will be unenforceable." She prayed that was the case. "Regardless, I rather feel like I've traded one prison for another."

Except she didn't suffer abuse in this prison, nor did she have to fear for her virtue.

"I know, little hen, but it's only temporary. I promise."

Until they were certain MacLerie had given up the chase, or she came of age. A mere week away. Not so very long to endure.

Leonidas cupped her chin, the pads of his fingers

slightly rough on her skin. "We just want you safe, and the risk is too great tonight."

At his warm touch, Primrose checked an involuntary, commanding urge to draw nearer until their chests and thighs met. His scent, his heat, his very presence beckoned to her on a level she couldn't comprehend but that went much deeper than physical attraction.

From that first day on the docks, when their eyes had met, a scintillating undercurrent had passed between them, and his spirit had touched hers.

Leonidas felt it too.

His eyes grew impossibly darker, the indigo of the ocean at twilight, and his focus dropped to her mouth.

Of their own volition, Primrose's lips parted in invitation.

"Primrose?"

"Aye?" Was that sultry voice hers?

She sounded positively wanton.

Chatting in the corridor made them spring apart like guilty children.

Grinning, Leonidas gave her a wicked wink.

"One of these days, I vow, I'm going to have that kiss, Primrose."

THIRTEEN

Hatchards Bookshop
187 Piccadilly

TWO HOURS LATER

Leonidas couldn't suppress his smile as Primrose gazed in awe at the myriad of books, magazines, journals, and almost everything a reader or writer could desire. He vowed not a single nook or cranny in the store's multiple floors had gone unexamined by her this past hour.

Observing her excitement brought him joy, and he couldn't regret putting aside his misgivings and allowing her this treat.

"The alphabet only has six and twenty letters, yet look

at all the works authors have cleverly written, and no two books are the same." She scrunched her pert nose, her hazel eyes alive with delight. "I'm sure you must have a tremendous sense of accomplishment that your books are available to purchase here."

"It is remarkable how clever humans are," he agreed. "And I'm grateful my writings have been well-received."

Wonder illuminating her face, Primrose strolled down an aisle, trailing her fingers over the books' spines. Three of Fletcher's bodyguards loitered within a few feet, each dressed in personal clothing rather than the suits required at *De la Chance.*

A casual observer wouldn't notice anything unusual unless they specifically watched Primrose and noticed the same three men shadowing her movements as she wandered around the establishment.

There hadn't been so much as a niggling of anything suspicious during the outing, and Leonidas relaxed a trifle. Perchance MacLerie had, indeed, given up the chase. In which case, Leonidas could depart England with much less concern about Primrose's safety.

Not that he had a date scheduled to leave yet.

His appointment with the harbormaster this morning hadn't proved productive.

In fact, Leonidas informed the patient chap to send a note 'round to *De la Chance* when a ship bound for Greece dropped anchor in the harbor. Until then, there was no point in him wasting more time hovering about the docks like a thief waiting to spring.

On a nearby aisle in the bookstore, a man chuckled and, elsewhere, a baby cooed. Whether young or aged, male or female, commoner or aristocrat, Hatchards had something for everyone, which is what made the place so popular.

Balancing a book in each of her palms, Primrose nibbled her lower lip with her teeth.

"I cannot decide between *Matilda; A Tale of the Day* and *The Conte di Carmagnola.*" She peeped upward through that thick fringe of gold-tipped lashes, the look almost teasing and seductive, although Leonidas was certain she didn't mean for her glance to be either.

Regardless, his male libido responded accordingly and, given the public setting, highly uncomfortably—an unanticipated reaction occurring often of late.

"I still want to select a book of travel as well," she murmured, turning the volumes this way and that as if they'd reveal a hidden secret that would help her determine which one to purchase.

"You don't have to buy them both now. We can always come another day."

Bollocks.

There Leonidas went again—offering to spend more time with her. It would only make it more difficult when he left. The rub was that with every passing day—*no, hour*—he became more reluctant to walk out of her life.

Had he taken leave of his senses?

Had a maggot crawled into his brain and warped his thinking?

Addled his mind?

What other explanation could there be?

Yes, he was dicked in the knob. Queer in the attic.

Then why was he so deuced happy and content?

Leonidas well knew the reason and wouldn't pretend otherwise. He genuinely enjoyed Primrose's company, and with each passing day, he became increasingly unwilling to board a ship and risk never seeing her again.

"True." After a moment's hesitation, Primrose slid *The Betrothed* back onto the shelf. As always, she wore no gloves.

Because she didn't own any or because she preferred not to, despite propriety?

Knowing Primrose as he'd come to these past weeks, likely both reasons were at play.

As she fell into step beside him, she cut him a sideways look—not quite coy, but not confident either. "What travel journal would you recommend?"

Leonidas furrowed his forehead, and then his expression cleared. "Since you had your heart set on traveling to Italy, Goethe's *Italian Journey*. You'll feel like you're right there with the author."

"It sounds positively divine." Smiling over her shoulder, she proceeded around the end of the aisle but came to such an abrupt halt that Leonidas bumped into her.

She tottered, and he steadied her by placing his hands on her delicate shoulders. When she'd regained her balance, he stepped backward a pace.

Not, however, before spying the cause of her hasty stop.

Frozen in place, undulating waves of fear pulsating from her, Primrose stared in dread at a distinguished man of middling years.

No one needed to tell Leonidas who he was.

Wallace MacLerie, Baron of Glentorquith.

The man Primrose had fled Scotland to escape.

Despite their precautions and diligence, the baron had found her, and Leonidas cursed inwardly for stupidly letting his guard down.

Instantly aware of the imminent danger, the bodyguards slipped into strategic positions.

The arrogant Scot flicked Leonidas a contemptuous glance, taking his measure from head to toe before dismissing him as one would a beggar. That said much about the man's opinion of himself and the power he wielded.

"Hello, Primrose, m'dear."

FOURTEEN

acLerie skewed his mouth into a cunning smile, his small, close-set eyes remaining cold and crafty. His thick burr raised Leonidas's hackles.

Primrose retreated until she came up against Leonidas. Quivering like a leaf buffeted by a gale's relentless wind, she shook her head. Her subtle floral scent wafted upward.

"How did ye find me?" she asked.

That she'd fallen into speaking with a Scots brogue testified to her terror.

"A letter arrived for ye from yer Aunt Shenton-Wayford's solicitor a couple of days after ye sneaked off. Seems she named ye in her will. Naturally, anything she bequeathed ye shall become mine once we exchange vows." A smug smile quirked the baron's mouth.

Leonidas wanted to punch the arrogant rotter into next December.

"I've come to take my bride home," MacLerie announced to no one in particular.

"Nae. I willna go with ye, Wallace MacLerie."

"Nae need to fash yerself or cause a fuss, *leannan*." Still wearing a self-important smile, MacLerie patted his coat. "I have the contract right here. I've done my due diligence. 'Tis legal and bindin'." He narrowed his beady eyes and flicked Leonidas what could only be interpreted as a warning glower. "*Even* in England."

Leonidas had his doubts as to that.

"It canna be," Primrose whispered, her face waxen. "I never agreed to the arrangement. And dinna call me sweetheart. I shall never be any such thing to ye."

Her terror ripped at Leonidas's heart, and removing her from the bloody blighter's presence became paramount.

"Come. Let's be away, Primrose." Leonidas took her elbow. "I'll send someone to make your purchases for you."

"I suggest ye unhand my betrothed." MacLerie glared daggers at Leonidas, and his comportment suggested the Scot would've run him through without hesitation had he possessed a sword. "I have nae qualms about involvin' the magistrate to retrieve what is mine."

"You do that, MacLerie." Leonidas regarded the pretentious prick with the same disgust he would week-old offal. "And when you do, be sure to tell him Miss McKessick is under the Westbrooks' protection."

MacLerie's bravado didn't falter a jot.

He flicked the bodyguards a dismissive glance, irritation causing the corners of his eyes to flex. Either he didn't recognize the Westbrook name or didn't care. The latter proved the more disturbing because that meant the rotter believed himself outside their realm of influence, which also probably meant he regarded himself as above the law.

How long had the belligerent buggar watched them in the store, waiting for the opportune moment to reveal himself?

Leonidas scanned the gathering crowd.

Did the Scot have men waiting in the midst, ready to do his bidding?

The situation could become ugly in the blink of an eye if MacLerie tried to take Primrose forcefully.

"Westbrook?" one of the intrigued onlookers murmured. "Isn't that the Duke of Latham's surname?"

"Aye. Only a maggot-pated numskull would cross His Grace," another put in.

"Move aside." The bystanders parted as Torrian Westbrook shoved his way through, wearing his perpetual grin. "I keep running into you at the most opportune times, Cousin."

"Indeed you do." Leonidas would vow this was no accidental meeting. Likely, Torrian had trailed them from *De la Chance* at Fletcher's behest in anticipation of something such as this.

Leonidas glanced behind Torrian, then leveled MacLerie a gloating grin. "We are leaving now. I trust you'll not want to take on mine and my cousin's men?"

Torrian's rugged agents stepped forward, and the crowd gasped.

His men were an impressive lot, and when Fletcher's bodyguards joined them, little doubt remained about who would leave the bookshop victorious.

"Mark my words, *sassenach*." MacLerie spat the word as if he'd a mouthful of manure. "This isnae over." Fury contorting his features, he fisted his hands. "I ken where Primrose is stayin', and I shall utilize the law to take what is mine."

"I'd rather die." Primrose had marshaled her composure and regained a portion of her spirit. "Which would likely conveniently happen should I nae provide ye with an heir just like yer previous wives."

"Watch yer mouth, wench." His expression thunderous, MacLerie leveled her a murderous glare. "Tamin' ye will be a pleasure I eagerly anticipate."

Over my dead body.

Leonidas shot the devil's spawn a squelching glare meant to incinerate him on the spot.

"Ignore him." Placing his hand on Primrose's slender back, and surrounded by the vigilant agents and bodyguards, Leonidas guided her from the shop to the waiting coach.

Gunter's visit would have to wait.

"Torrian, I would have a word with you," he said as two of Fletcher's men climbed onto the driver's seat and a pair of Torrian's took up positions as tigers on the rear.

His cousin nodded.

Leonidas handed Primrose into the coach, and she sank weakly onto the bench. "I'll be but a minute."

Her faint nod and haunted eyes eviscerated him.

There was no way in hell Leonidas would ever allow MacLerie to take or marry her.

Leonidas intended to make certain of it.

Primrose would never have to fear the baron again.

He motioned to Torrian and spoke low.

"Are you certain?" His cousin jerked his head up, disbelief and concern etching his face. "That seems a mite excessive, if you don't mind my saying so."

"Positive." Leonidas gave a stern dip of his chin. "As soon as possible."

"Very well." Torrian slung an arm around Leonidas's shoulder. "I'll see to the details as soon as I've seen you safely to *De la Chance*."

Leonidas climbed inside the coach and, rather than sitting across from Primrose, sat beside her.

She turned her face away, but not before he saw tears glistening on her dewy cheeks.

"Come here, little hen." He gathered her into his arms and held her as she wept. "All will be well. Trust me."

"How can it be?" she mumbled into his coat.

Her vulnerability ripped his heart open.

"What if he is telling the truth and the law *is* on his side?" She shuddered. "I'd rather die than marry that revolting toad."

The coach lurched into motion.

"It shan't come to that," Leonidas assured her. "I have a foolproof plan."

A hastily hatched scheme which meant he would not be sailing for Greece. He willingly released that goal for now because the truth was that nothing—absolutely nothing—was more important to him at this moment than Primrose.

She released a shaky laugh. "I'm doubtful that even a Westbrook can disregard the law."

Cuddling her close, he kissed her temple.

"You cannot marry the toad if you are already married."

FIFTEEN

A DOZEN IRREGULAR HEARTBEATS LATER

Certain her jaw sagged to her chin and her eyes had grown round as dual moons or that she resembled a beached cod fish, Primrose leaned away and gaped at Leonidas. Curling her hands into fists, she snapped her mouth closed, shut her eyes, and counted to five.

Then counted to five again.

And a third time before forcing her eyelids open.

Wariness and amusement vied for supremacy in his azure gaze as he regarded her—*the confounded, enigmatic man*.

When Primrose could finally trust herself to speak without sounding like a Bedlam lunatic or a drunken harpy, she choked out, "Married? To who?"

Or was it whom?

What did it matter?

When she'd first arrived at *De la Chance*, she'd wondered if she'd jumped from the proverbial frying pan into the fire.

She had her answer.

A shadow flitted across Leonidas's face, or perchance they'd passed beneath a cloud, darkening the coach's interior further.

"Me, of course. Who else?"

Who else indeed?

"By special license this afternoon," he said. "I sent Torrian to acquire one."

A wave of pure panic sluiced through Primrose.

"You cannot be serious, Leonidas."

Is this what drowning felt like?

Struggling to stay afloat when far stronger forces sucked you under?

What other catastrophic surprises portending calamity would this infernal day bring?

He folded his arms, causing the biceps to bulge against the fabric of his coat. "I assure you. I am absolutely serious."

"But we barely know each other." Marriages of convenience and arranged marriages were common for the wealthy and aristocracy. Even Mama's unfortunate union had been a marriage of convenience on her part and a seized opportunity on Lyster's, who'd lusted after her for years.

"You're an English duke's son," she pointed out unnecessarily. "I'm a Scottish commoner, the result of rape."

Yes, English blueblood ran in her veins, but Primrose had never considered Mama's treacherous family kin.

Class-difference marriages were rare, and usually occurred because the couple was madly in love and willing to eschew Society's rules.

A myriad of other truths marched across Primrose's mind.

You don't love me.

I do not know if I love you.

You're leaving England—perhaps for years.

Marriage is forever. It would be a long-term solution to a temporary problem.

Granted, a very troublesome and highly disconcerting problem, but couldn't she hide somewhere safe for another few days until she turned one and twenty?

"You know station means nothing to me, Primrose. I prefer to judge a person by their character, not a label."

She folded her arms and returned his glower before issuing an unladylike snort that, rather than causing him to raise a noble brow in askance, made the corners of his sexy mouth twitch.

Skepticism arched an eyebrow high on her forehead. Her tone dry as ashes, she said, "I'm sure your father and mother, the duke and duchess, would feel *much* differently."

"No, they would not," he denied, warmth shining from his eyes, causing her insides to flutter in such a disturbing manner that it made staying stern and logical deucedly difficult. "Althelia's husband is a bastard. Lucius's wife is Spanish, and Adolphus's is French. Both women have, shall we say, *colorful* pasts."

What, precisely, did *colorful* mean?

A wheel sank into a hole, jostling Primrose on the seat and jarring her musings to more important matters— specifically, MacLerie's intentions.

She bit her lip. "Under English law, would the marriage be valid? I don't have parental consent."

In truth, she wasn't positive MacLerie wouldn't resort to abduction or forcing himself on her even after she'd come of age in a week. The man was obsessed and had crossed into lunacy. He wanted Primrose and meant to have her by any means, fair or foul.

Leonidas shrugged. "You're of age in a few days. We can simply recite vows again if need be. At least, by wedding, we will delay MacLerie until you are one and twenty. Even if he's susceptible to bribery, no magistrate is going to haul a Westbrook bride off and risk the wrath of the church and my father."

The coach trundled along, its wheels grinding on the cobblestones. Outside, pedestrians, riders, and other conveyances passed by as if all was right in the world.

It was not.

Not only had MacLerie found Primrose and threatened to take her by force, but Leonidas had gone stark-raving mad.

Marry him.

Primrose would have to be utterly addled or completely desperate.

She wasn't the former, and though MacLerie had frightened her, she couldn't exchange vows with a man she'd known a mere three weeks.

Leonidas turned her hand over, tracing his forefinger across the groves there. The motion proved surprisingly comforting and perhaps the teeniest erotic.

"I know it's a shock, Primrose, but put aside your emotions if you can and consider this logically. I don't believe MacLerie will ever give up his pursuit of you. Do you?"

She gave a grudging shake of her head. "Nae."

Leonidas's words mirrored her thoughts of moments before.

"I think he's deranged." A shudder rippled over her as

she imagined the horror of being his wife. His hands on her. No, she couldn't bear it.

"If he manages to convince the authorities he has a legal right to you and that we are keeping you from him—a real possibility if he lines the right pockets—*De la Chance* could be raided." Tension hardened the chiseled contours of Leonidas's face. "Even with Fletcher's bodyguards and the Westbrooks' influence, we might not be able to prevent him from taking you, and we could have charges brought against us."

"But I'm at *De la Chance* willingly." Puckering her forehead, Primrose absently watched the mesmerizing trail he drew on her palm. "No one is keeping me there or preventing me from leaving."

Except her circumstances, that was.

Leonidas's indigo eyes gleamed with cynicism and compassion. "That wouldn't matter to a corrupt official with heavily greased palms. I assure you, London is full of them."

"So is Scotland." Her heart heavy, Primrose forced herself to analyze the situation rationally.

"We might only have hours, perhaps a day or two, until MacLerie shows up with reinforcements. The only other solution is for you to leave." He brushed a finger along her jaw, and she wanted to close her eyes and press into his caress.

She wasn't immune to Leonidas—far from it.

But to marry him?

Tie herself to him for a lifetime while he gallivanted around the world?

"However, you told me you have nowhere to go," he reminded her gently. "No family or friends."

"I don't." Her mother's immediate family assuredly would not take her in. Mama's parents and siblings had cut her off, and she'd never heard from them again. After a decade, Mama had finally stopped writing to them. Their cold-blooded rejection had shattered her already broken heart.

Why was it that good fortune fell into the laps of some, and others like Mama always toiled and suffered? And why did women often receive the blame and suffer the consequences for men's reprehensible actions?

Because, as Leonidas had just pointed out, unscrupulous men with affluence possessed power and thus exerted control.

"I thought you were a confirmed bachelor." Angling her head, Primrose searched his face. "Precisely what would this union look like?"

Not that she truly entertained any notion of exchanging vows with him.

Nevertheless, curiosity drove her to ask.

"True, I never anticipated wedding, but giving you my name is the only viable option I see to keep you safe." Leaning back, Leonidas crossed his long legs. "Naturally,

I'll continue as I always have with traveling and writing but shall provide for you."

Of course he would.

That answered that question.

Primrose arched a starchy eyebrow. "And what am *I* to do while you are rambling around the world?"

She couldn't help but notice Leonidas hadn't invited her to accompany him, even though he knew she wanted to travel.

His easy grin held a touch of indulgence, and his condescension irked her.

Her question wasn't unreasonable.

"Stay on at *De la Chance* if you wish." He rubbed his nose. "I doubt Fletcher would object. Or, if you prefer, I can set you up with a house in your chosen location."

In truth, Primrose had no idea where she'd like to live.

She still doubted that MacLerie would respect a marriage license. Nevertheless, he also needed an heir. Perhaps he might direct his noxious attentions toward another unfortunate female—God help the poor thing.

"Other than perhaps assuring my safety, why would I consent to such an arrangement and become your chattel? You'll continue to do what you've always intended, Leonidas, while I must relinquish my dreams of someday marrying for love and having children."

Not that she'd entertained that fantasy of late.

Leonidas's voice grew deep and raspy, and his smoldering gaze sent heat scorching up her face. "*We* could have children."

Every bone in Primrose's body threatened to turn to custard.

She floundered for a response that would cool his ardor and hers.

"For me to raise alone? No, thank you, Leonidas. Call me old-fashioned, but I believe children need both parents in their lives."

Eyebrows pulled together, he studied the coach's far corner. A muscle ticked in his jaw, and Primrose realized he was angry, though carefully controlling his irritation.

"I shan't give up traveling and exploring to play nurse-maid." He swung his attention back to her, and the hard coolness in his eyes hitched her breath. "I believe it's sacrifice enough to offer you my name and protection."

How magnanimous.

She bit her tongue against a stinging retort.

They were at a crossroads.

"You're suggesting a marriage of convenience." Not so very different than the marriage Lyster had arranged, except Primrose could tolerate Leonidas. Much more than tolerate, truth be told. "We'd live separate lives? Have discreet liaisons? We're *both* free to do as we please?"

At his censorious look, she shrugged.

"I simply want to make sure I understand *what* exactly

the arrangement would entail, Leonidas. Dalliances are common in most marriages of convenience."

Primrose believed in the sanctity of marriage vows and would never commit adultery, but he didn't know that.

Leonidas's nostrils flared the merest bit before he spoke in a carefully tempered tenor. "I would not tolerate infidelity, Primrose, so rid yourself of that notion. Nor would ours be a marriage in name only. The union shall be consummated."

Her pulse quickened at the desire momentarily sparking in his blue eyes.

Ah, so she must remain faithful, live alone for years at a time, entertain his physical desires, all to prevent a madman from dragging her back to Scotland.

It didn't seem like a fair exchange.

The coach drew up before *De la Chance*. Dark shadows outside and heavy, pewter clouds portended another rainstorm. Somehow, the petulant weather seemed appropriate for the day.

Primrose shifted toward the door. "I shall need time to consider your offer."

"You have until half of three." Leonidas pressed the door latch. "That's when the cleric is to arrive at the club to perform the ceremony."

"*Half three*? But that's only a couple of hours from now." Panic sluiced through her.

It was too soon.

How could she decide on something so momentous in such a short time?

This was her life—her entire future at stake.

Leonidas hopped from the coach, then turned to face her, his expression inscrutable.

"I promise you, Primrose. I'm no more thrilled about the prospect than you are. Marriage was never on my horizon."

"Thank you for clarifying your grudging proposal," she snapped, her patience and equanimity at an end. "I regret being an imposition and inconvenience."

To his credit, Leonidas didn't respond to her peevishness, though the granite line of his jaw revealed he wasn't unaffected by her scold.

"Nevertheless, marrying is the only way I know to protect you." He roved that indigo gaze over her face. "If you decide to accept my offer, the ceremony will be in the private salon."

He turned on his heels and entered the building without a backward glance.

SIXTEEN

De la Chance's Private Salon

FORTY MINUTES PAST THREE

*S*he's late. She's not coming.

For the umpteenth time, Leonidas cut a brief glance at the Empire mantel clock before examining the salon's open door. He wiped clammy palms on his immaculate black coat—his finest.

Despite the circumstances, reciting vows called for appropriate attire.

He blamed his moist palms on the blazing fire in the hearth to dispel the chill caused by the fresh onslaught of rain outdoors. He refused to consider anything else—

assuredly not nerves or anticipation—had induced the dampness.

As if the occasion called for it, Fletcher had tucked a peach rose into his lapel fifteen minutes ago when he'd entered the salon. Surprisingly, his brother hadn't lectured him on the insanity of marrying a woman he'd only known three weeks. Nor had Fletcher tried to talk him out of taking Primrose to wife, both of which Leonidas had prepared defensive arguments for.

His brother, Torrian, the bald-pated, rose-cheeked, cheerful rector, and a half dozen others talked in low tones. Evidently, Fletcher had been of the same mind as Leonidas.

The more witnesses, the better, just in case MacLerie tried to contest the marriage.

Leonidas didn't miss the frequent glances of those assembled toward the clock, the conspicuously empty doorway, or toward him.

Pity tempered those last gazes, which irked him to no end.

It wasn't as if he was a love-sick swain jilted at the altar.

He'd given Primrose a clear choice.

Plainly, her answer was no.

In all honestly, Leonidas didn't blame her.

That didn't lessen the problem with MacLerie, however.

Fletcher approached and, after clasping Leonidas's shoulder, murmured, "I fear Primrose's tardiness is my fault. I sent Fiona, Suzannah, and Teresa to help her prepare for the ceremony. A suitable gown, styling her hair, and flowers. A parure set as a wedding gift from me. I've asked Mrs. Dough to prepare an appropriate meal for afterward."

"Seems you've been awfully busy, big brother." Leonidas cocked his head. "I'm not sure whether to thank you or take exception at your presumptuousness."

"Oh, definitely thank me." A half-grin tugging his mouth upward on one side, Fletcher shrugged. "Besides, every woman deserves a nice wedding, even if the preparations are done in haste."

Was Fletcher's generosity and kindness the reason Primrose was tardy?

"You don't mind?" Leonidas might as well get that awkward business out in the open. "I thought you might harbor an interest in Primrose yourself."

If Fletcher offered to take his place, could Leonidas retreat with graciousness?

Something inside him howled a denial at the idea.

"No, not a bit of it. Although I admit, Primrose is an exceptional woman." Shaking his head, his brother chuckled. Fleeting chagrin swept across Fletcher's face. "In truth, I hoped to make her more enticing for you, hence the pretty gowns. Scented soaps. Permission to borrow my books when I know you use this salon as an office when you are here."

Relief tempered with a good deal of irritation engulfed Leonidas.

"You are a manipulating devil, Fletcher Westbrook."

"I suspected your interest in Primrose from the beginning. You'd never have brought her here or have offered her marriage if you were immune to her." Fletcher poked Leonidas's chest over his heart. "I think you know that in there, even if you cannot admit it to yourself yet."

Since when had Fletcher grown philosophical?

Leonidas rubbed his chin. "Well, it doesn't look like my bride—"

A collective gasp drew his attention, and he pivoted to look in the direction the others stared.

Nothing could have prepared him for the blinding vision of loveliness who brought his thoughts to a crashing halt.

Primrose stood in the entry, flanked by the women who'd helped her prepare for her wedding, and God help him, her beauty took his breath away.

She was, in a word, perfection.

Leonidas's heart fairly sang for joy.

She's mine. She's mine.

For all time. Primrose is mine.

Pink and yellow rosebuds tucked into her Grecian coiffure complemented the coral gown she wore with its delicate lace overskirt embroidered with pink, peach, and yellow roses. Peach beaded slippers peeked out from beneath the hem, and a coral and pearl necklace caressed her neck while matching earrings dangled from her delicate earlobes. The small bouquet she clutched in her lace-gloved hands also contained pink, yellow, and peach roses.

How Fletcher had managed to pull this together in the few hours since Leonidas and Primrose had returned from Hatchards was nothing short of miraculous. Of course, it was most convenient that the decorations for the country dancing tonight just happened to match the wedding theme.

Becoming color tinting her porcelain cheeks, Primrose glided into the room.

Clasping the *Book of Common Prayer* to his chest, Reverend Honeywell cleared his throat. "Shall we begin the solemnization of matrimony then?"

Leonidas crossed to her.

"Primrose. Are you ready?"

She nodded, and he tucked her trembling hand into the crook of his arm and guided her to stand before the reverend. The others formed a semi-circle around them, and the cleric began the ceremony.

His focus on Primrose at his side, Leonidas only half-listened.

Her skin the color of lilies, she trembled and swallowed several times.

He understood her nervousness. Even his heart palpitated, and his blood fairly raced through his veins.

Reverend Honeywell peered at Leonidas above his spectacles.

"Leonidas Rafe Desmond Westbrook, wilt thou have this woman to thy wedded wife, to live together after God's ordinance in the holy estate of matrimony? Wilt thou love her, comfort her, honor, and keep her, in sickness and in health; and, forsaking all others, keep thee only unto her, so long as you both shall live?"

Primrose stiffened, her breath coming in shallow little pants.

Fearing she might swoon, Leonidas glanced downward.

Primrose stared straight ahead, her pallor waxen.

"I shall." He gave her hand a reassuring squeeze.

The reverend switched his attention to Primrose.

"Primrose Crystabel Faye McKessick, wilt thou have this man to thy wedded husband, to live together after God's ordinance in the holy estate of matrimony? Wilt thou obey him, and serve him, love, honor, and keep him, in sickness and in health; and, forsaking all others, keep thee only unto him, so long as you both shall live?"

Primrose opened her mouth, but no sound came out.

She turned her stricken gaze upward, meeting Leonidas's eyes.

A tear leaked from the corner of her eye and trailed ever-so-slowly down her smooth cheek.

Leonidas knew what she would say before she uttered the barely audible words, and the cleaving pain nearly gutted him.

"I canna do this, Leonidas. It wouldna be fair to either of us. Marriage shouldna be a convenient solution. I'd be robbin' both of us of the opportunity for true love. Someday, ye'll see that I'm right."

Clasping a hand to her mouth, she fled the room.

SEVENTEEN

Fletcher's Office

FOUR DAYS LATER – EARLY AFTERNOON

Her stomach twisted into a tangled knot, Primrose knocked on Fletcher's office door. This summons wasn't unexpected either, although she'd anticipated he would have chosen to speak with her sooner.

Surely, she'd put her employer in an untenable position by refusing to marry his brother and protect herself and everyone at *De la Chance* from Wallace MacLerie's vindictiveness.

She barely ate or slept for dread that the baron would descend upon *De la Chance* any moment, the authorities in tow. That he hadn't appeared yet was as much a reprieve as unnerving. She didn't believe for a second that he'd given up the chase.

His pride wouldn't allow him to.

"Come in," Fletcher bid.

Leonidas wouldn't be here this time.

This morning, Sean informed her that Leonidas had received a long-awaited message from the harbormaster. No doubt the young man thought Primrose would welcome the news that Leonidas would sail to Greece soon.

She should have done.

After all, she'd rejected his marriage offer—at the altar, no less.

So why did her heart feel like a team of draft horses had trampled it?

Still, Primrose couldn't regret her decision.

It was what was best for them both, despite her remorse and his humiliation.

Perhaps in time, Leonidas would come to not only understand her decision but to appreciate it.

Lifting her chin in a show of bravado, more for herself than for Fletcher, she pressed the handle and slipped into the room.

Fletcher glanced up, his expression unreadable. He angled his chin toward an armchair.

"Please have a seat, Primrose. I must finish this correspondence."

She did as he bid and folded her hands in the lap of her emerald-green gown.

A frown of concentration creating a crease above his nose, Fletcher scribbled away, his pen scritching across the foolscap. He finished with a flourishing signature and, after returning the pen to its holder, sprinkled sand across the wet ink and pushed the letter aside to dry.

He leaned back in his chair. "Torrian brought news this morning that I believe you should be aware of."

Her blood ran cold, then hot.

So this was it then.

Primrose plucked at the material of her gown. "I presume MacLerie found favor with the authorities."

Fletcher had no choice but to dismiss her.

For the safety of his other employees as well as his continued business operation.

She didn't begrudge him his decision.

Somehow, she'd get by.

She would ask Fletcher for her wages to date and meant to contact Aunt Rhodesia's solicitor and inquire about the bequeathment, but she didn't know his name.

Given Chesley's desperation for funds, Aunt Rhodesia's final gift would likely be a token. Nevertheless, it touched her heart that her grandaunt had thought of her.

"No." Fletcher leaned forward, resting his forearms on his desk.

"*Nae?*"

Fletcher shook his dark head.

Then this meeting was about Leonidas.

"There's no pretty way to say this, Primrose."

"I'd prefer forthrightness." No beating around the bush. No platitudes or trying to soften the blow.

"As do I." After scrutinizing her for a lengthy moment, he gave a tight nod. "The night before last, there was a violent altercation at a west-end brothel. The details are unclear, but it appears some women, pushed to their limits, coordinated a rebellion of sorts."

"Och, I'm sure they had just cause." Primrose would not judge them, but what had that to do with her? And why had Fletcher thought it important enough to summon her to his office?

"I agree." He pulled his earlobe. "The long and short of it is that a fire ensued, and Hadleigh and several patrons perished, as did the madame and four prostitutes."

"*Guid* Lord." Primrose pitied the women but felt only liberated that Hadleigh had met his maker and would reside in hell for eternity. As for the patrons, well, they preyed upon vulnerable women. She couldn't feel sorry for them, though she pitied their families.

"MacLerie was among those killed. Torrian confirmed

his identity this morning." His expression intent, Fletcher leaned forward again. "Primrose, you are free of him, once and for all."

Choking on a gasp, Primrose collapsed back into the chair. Tears burned behind her eyelids, not of grief but of profound reprieve.

"Och, I'm free of him." Her voice shook. "Really free."

De la Chance was no longer in danger either.

"Indeed, you are." Satisfaction laced Fletcher's voice as he folded the now-dry letter and tucked it into a drawer. "However, there is another matter I wish to speak with you about."

"I'm sorry, Fletcher, but I won't discuss what happened with Leonidas. That's between him and me." Primrose hadn't seen him since that awful afternoon. "I shall only say that a rushed union would not have made either of us happy. We'd have always wondered if the other would've chosen us had we not been forced into the match. Doubt can erode relationships, and I wanted more than that for both of us."

"Hold there." Fletcher held up his hands, palms outward. "I couldn't agree with you more, and I don't intend to talk about that. Although I shall tell you the same thing I told my brother."

Curious despite herself, Primrose tilted her head. "And that is?"

"I suspect you sensed something between you, else you wouldn't have trusted Leonidas to bring you here or even have dressed for the wedding. A part of you wanted to go through with the ceremony."

Fletcher had the right of it, but Primrose didn't want to discuss her conflicted emotions. If she spoke to anyone about her feelings, it should be Leonidas.

But he was leaving, and when he sailed through the Bay of Biscay, cruised along the Western coast of France and Spain, passed through the Strait of Gibraltar, and crossed into the Mediterranean Sea, he'd take her fractured heart with him, though he'd never know it.

Primrose *might've* researched the most common route from England to Greece.

She did yearn to travel, after all.

What a glorious time Leonidas would have.

She was happy for him.

Truly.

"What is it then, Fletcher?"

She sneaked a glance at the clock.

Nearly half of three.

Suzannah, Teresa, and Fiona had invited her to join them for afternoon tea for the past two days. It seemed she'd somehow won their approval by *not* marrying Leonidas.

"At Leonidas's behest, I asked Torrian to find out who your Aunt Shenton-Wayford's solicitor is. Leonidas mentioned the attorney had sent a letter to Scotland for you. I've arranged for Mr. Thorburn Watchit to meet you here at half-three."

"I don't know what to say except thank you." Even after she'd rejected Leonidas, Fletcher continued to be kind, not spiteful.

A knock echoed at the door.

"Right on time." Fletcher grinned before calling, "Yes?"

Chandler opened the door and poked his head inside. "Mr. Watchit is here, Mr. Westbrook."

"Show him in." Fletcher stood, as did Primrose. "I'll allow you privacy. Take all the time you need. I have a meeting at *Ivories and Aces* all afternoon."

Tall and wiry, Mr. Watchit strolled in, his expression amiable but keen and assessing as it rested upon her. "Miss Primrose McKessick, I presume?"

"Yes." Primrose nodded. "And you are Mr. Watchit."

Fletcher left, shutting the door behind him.

"I confess, I didn't expect to find you in England, Miss McKessick, but it makes my job much easier." His face crumpled into a fatherly smile. "Do have a seat. This shan't take long."

Primrose sank onto the chair as the solicitor dragged documents from his time-worn briefcase.

He thumbed through the first couple of pages.

"Ah, here it is." He met her curious gaze. "You have

been bequeathed a house in Kensington, eight thousand pounds, and several valuable pieces of jewelry, which are currently held in a safe at my office."

"*Pardon?*" Primrose almost poked her fingers in her ears to ensure she'd heard correctly. "Did you say...? Chesley didn't inherit everything?"

"Not these." Mr. Watchit shook his head, his smile widening. "This bequeathment was given into your aunt's safekeeping by your maternal grandmother, the now deceased Viscountess Florinda Tierney, to be held for you. Your aunt fretted her wayward son would avail himself of the money and jewels and entrusted them to my care until you came of age." Eyes twinkling, he said, "Which, according to my records, is in three days. Is that correct?"

"I turn one and twenty on the thirtieth." Dazed and overwhelmed, Primrose put a hand to her forehead. "Do I understand you correctly? My maternal grandmother left me a house, jewels, and money?"

Why hadn't the viscountess helped Mama?

"There's a letter from your grandmother as well." Mr. Watchit came around the desk. "I just need your signature here, Miss McKessick. Then everything can be released to you."

Her mind reeling and unable to quite comprehend the turn of events, Primrose signed the document.

Mr. Watchit shoved another set of papers toward her.

"These are your copies. The letter from your grandmother is amongst them."

"Thank you." She collected the small stack.

In the past fifteen minutes, she went from being a near pauper pursued by a madman and a pimp to a wealthy young woman.

Only one thing would make Primrose's life perfect.

If Leonidas loved her.

"Congratulations, Miss McKessick." With practiced efficiency, he returned the other papers to his briefcase. "I'll deliver the deed, jewelry, and money to you next week if that is acceptable."

"Yes, that will be fine." She needn't stay on at *De la Chance* if she didn't wish to. But she probably would because, occasionally, she might catch a glimpse of Leonidas.

The solicitor slipped from the room, and Primrose fumbled with the papers until she found the letter from her grandmother, still sealed with the family crest pressed into green wax.

Bracing herself, she cracked the seal and read the short missive from the grandmother she'd never known. Afterward, she covered her face with her hands and wept.

Wept for her mama, who had never known how much her mother grieved being forbidden to speak to her daughter. Wept for the viscountess who found a way to help the grandchild she'd been denied. And Primrose wept for herself because now she could do what she'd dreamed of for so long. And in the end, they didn't matter because she'd denied herself the one thing she'd always want.

Leonidas.

"I'm sorry," she whispered into her fingers. "I'm so sorry."

EIGHTEEN

Still in Fletcher's Study

Leonidas squatted before Primrose and touched her knee. "*Shh*, little hen."

She jerked her head up, her dear face ravaged by tears.

"I knocked, but no one answered," he explained. "I thought the office was empty."

Her pulse beat a frantic tempo at the juncture of her throat and collarbone.

With his thumbs, he wiped the tears from her cheeks. "What has you so distraught?"

She motioned to the papers but succumbed to another bout of weeping.

He lifted her into his arms and carried her to the sofa.

In truth, he'd almost turned around and left when he'd spied her sobbing. Her grief cleaved his heart from his chest, but he hadn't come to grips with her refusing to marry him. Though if he were perfectly honest, she'd displayed courage and integrity by refusing a match many women would've jumped at.

After settling onto a cushion, Leonidas cradled her in his arms and ran his hands over her back and shoulders as she wept. Several long minutes passed with only the clock's *tick-tocking* and the fire's spitting and snapping punctuating the tranquil silence.

Finally, she drew in a shuddery breath and lifted her damp face with those enormous eyes fringed with spiky eyelashes to search his eyes.

So help him, Leonidas couldn't have stopped himself from lowering his lips to hers, even had he wanted to. And God knew he didn't want to. Before he left her life for good, he must have one taste of her sweet lips to last him a lifetime.

Settling his mouth over Primrose's, he poured every unspoken sentiment, every longing, every heart's desire into the caress. At first, she didn't respond, then she sighed, relaxed into his embrace, and opened her mouth in invitation.

His soul soared with joy as he tenderly explored the depths of her mouth.

His body demanded he slake his lust, but he tamped down the carnal urge.

This was Primrose.

She might never be his, but he'd treasure her in his heart until his dying day. Wherever he went in the world, Primrose would be stamped upon his soul, etched into his spirit.

Wrestling his passion under control, Leonidas dropped a final kiss on her swollen lips and rearranged her so that she sat beside him. Her tempting bottom moving atop his groin proved too painful to continue. He prayed she didn't notice his erection.

Taking her delicate fingers in his, he pressed his mouth to the knuckles. He kissed an ink stain on her thumb.

"We have this in common." He displayed the dark blotches upon his fingers.

Her half-smile wrung his heart. "I thought you were at the docks arranging passage."

"I was. It didn't take as long as I expected." The anticipation he'd experienced less than a month ago no longer drove him. "May I ask why you were crying?"

She pointed to Fletcher's desk.

"My Aunt Rhodesia's solicitor was just here. It seems I owe you another debt of gratitude, Leonidas."

"How so?" He canted his head.

"My maternal grandmother left me a sizeable inheritance, which I shall receive on my birthday. There was also a letter explaining why she cut my mother off. Her husband, the viscount, had forced her to, but she defied him and left me what she'd inherited from her mother's family."

"I'm glad of it." Leonidas swept a curl off her forehead. "What will you do now?"

Gazing into the fire, Primrose lifted a shapely shoulder. "I haven't decided. I don't want to rush into anything."

Leonidas winced at her unintentional mention of that disastrous afternoon that had left a lasting mark on his soul and pride.

"Fletcher also told me that MacLerie is dead." She wrinkled her nose. "I *wasn't* crying about that, though the circumstances were awful."

Leonidas chuckled and tugged a fair curl. "Torrian informed me this morning before I left."

"You'll sail soon?" Primrose brought her gaze to meet his. Sorrow and resignation pooled in the hazel-blue depths.

No sense delaying the inevitable.

"On the thirtieth with the evening tide." Why wasn't he elated? "I've taken rooms near the docks so that I can concentrate on my writing."

That was a bald-faced lie.

He'd taken rooms because seeing Primrose every day and knowing she'd never be his eviscerated him.

A log shifted in the hearth, sending crimson sparks flying up the chimney.

If Primrose suspected Leonidas's departure from *De la Chance* prior to sailing was due to her, she hid it well.

She nodded. "That is good. Because of me, you've been delayed nearly a month. I don't suppose...? Would it...?" Pressing her lips together, Primrose shook her head and averted her gaze. "Never mind."

"What is it, little hen?" Leonidas captured her chin between his thumb and forefinger, gently forcing her to meet his eyes. "You know you can ask me anything."

"I wondered if you might write me of your adventures."

Leonidas couldn't help but feel she asked for something else too.

"I can, though I'm a horrible correspondent." He gave a self-deprecating grin. "How ironic that I can write an entire book but struggle to fill a single page for a letter."

It was true.

Leonidas's parents and siblings forever despaired of him writing regularly.

"It's of no import." Wistfulness softened her features. "Perhaps I'll travel now too."

It was on the tip of Leonidas's tongue to ask her to accompany him as his wife, but he squelched the urge. He was fairly certain that her feelings toward him had not changed markedly in four days. That knowledge stung because one undeniable truth had cudgeled him as he'd watched her flee the parlor.

Leonidas loved Primrose.

And because he loved her, he wouldn't remain at *De la Chance* until he sailed. A man could only stand so much torment.

He who had never wanted to marry, who didn't believe love was a part of his future, had fallen in love with a spirited Scottish lass. As certain as he was that February followed January, he would never love another.

He supposed it was good that he'd already determined to remain a bachelor.

Primrose stirred, and he released her hand.

"Thank you for everything, Leonidas." Her turbulent gaze belied her calm smile as she stood. "You quite literally saved me, and now I have much to look forward to. If you think of me, please know I'm forever grateful."

Leonidas didn't want Primrose's gratitude.

He wanted *her*.

"Goodbye, Leonidas." She brushed her fingertips over his cheek and then glided from the room. And his life.

And he let her go.

Because if there was one thing he'd learned about Primrose McKessick, she treasured her freedom above all else.

NINETEEN

De la Chance's Ballroom

30 MAY – LATE EVENING

Though her heart pained her with every beat, Primrose forced her lips to remain bent upward as she received another birthday greeting. Somehow, word had spread at the ball that she celebrated her first and twentieth birthday today.

She strongly suspected one or all of the trio, as she'd come to think of Suzannah, Fiona, and Teresa, had let the secret slip. Now that no further danger existed, Fletcher had insisted Primrose attend the ball as a guest to celebrate her coming of age.

She dreamed of attending a grand ball like this as a

little girl. Now that she had, she couldn't enjoy herself, for every moment, she longed for Leonidas.

His twinkling dark blue eyes. That shock of midnight hair that fell over his noble brow. The ready upward sweep of his well-molded mouth. Those same lips moving upon hers.

She put a finger to her lips before realizing what she was doing and hastily lowered her hand.

She'd grown fond of Fletcher in a purely brotherly manner.

Every now and again, she'd catch a glimpse of him and, for an instant, think it was Leonidas. Her heart would stall and then accelerate in joy before reality came crashing down around her.

Leonidas left just as he said he would.

Even had they exchanged vows, he would have gone.

She knew that to be true, and yet, wasn't a glass half full better than an empty glass?

How could she miss him so much already?

Primrose curled her hand into her gown's fabric and released it at once, else she would wrinkle the silk.

Since she had nothing elegant to wear to such a prestigious event, and there'd been no time to have a new gown sewn, she'd reluctantly donned what was to have been her wedding gown.

Such a wave of anguish pummeled her, she bit her lip from crying out.

Leonidas had sailed away tonight.

Even now, he was on his way out to sea.

Primrose kept hoping he'd say something, *anything*, to reveal he felt more than physical attraction toward her. That something other than obligation, honor, or wanting to protect her had motivated him to marry her.

Those reasons were all good and noble, but not what a woman charging headlong into an unforeseen marriage wanted to hear. Except after that afternoon when they'd shared that blissful, soul-shattering kiss, she hadn't seen him again.

He hadn't said what she longed to hear, and she hadn't been brave enough to share her love after she'd quite literally run from him while exchanging their wedding vows. Her love prevented her from saying, "I shall," and trapping him into an unwanted union.

Now, she stood here in this gorgeous gown with its tormenting memories and regret as her only companion as she faced a long, lonely future.

"Why the long face, Primrose?" Teresa sidled up to her, stunning as ever in a black ballgown.

"'Tis nothing. I'm simply not accustomed to this falderol as you are." Primrose managed what she hoped was a cheerful smile. "I imagine I'll adjust."

Thank goodness Mama had taught her several dances so she wouldn't make a complete fool of herself, though she was horribly out of practice. Laboring from dawn until late evening didn't leave much time to perfect dance steps.

Suzannah joined them, vigorously waving her black brisé fan before her flushed face.

"I only have a moment. I promised Lord Baltimore the next dance." She curled her perfect nose. "I may have to demand a pay raise. The old goat smells of cheese and camphor, and he has wandering hands."

Across the room, Fiona gave a little hand wave before rolling her eyes ceilingward as she pasted a smile on her face and greeted the impossibly clumsy and awkward but extremely well-heeled and connected Dawson Jefferson.

"Ta ta." Suzannah floated away, the picture of elegance, and accepted the arm of a hunch-backed, knobby-kneed older gentleman.

"I had no idea what you endured at these dances," Primrose murmured.

As her position didn't require her to provide entertainment, which included dancing with partnerless men as the trio did, she'd been spared the same fate.

"It's not that bad." Teresa patted her glossy hair. "Mr. Westbrook and his men ensure the guests behave themselves. If they don't, they are tossed out on their arses and are not allowed to return. Excuse me, I promised this dance too."

Making her way to the refreshment table, Primrose circumvented the crowd of at least two hundred. Though the doors stood open on either end of the ballroom, the atmosphere proved beastly hot, and she was in dire need of a glass of lemonade or ratafia.

She selected a glass from the table and lifted it to her lips. The sweet yet tart liquid trailed down her dry throat.

How much longer must she stay in order not to offend Fletcher?

As promised, Mr. Watchit had delivered the deed to her house, a jewelry box full of exquisite jewels, and the money this afternoon. Fletcher had offered to put everything in his safe, which she had gratefully accepted.

Until Primrose decided what to do, she intended to remain at *De la Chance*.

Out of the corner of her eye, she caught sight of a familiar head.

Leonidas?

It's not him. He sailed with the tide.

Nonetheless, Primrose turned, hoping against hope she'd see her beloved.

Fletcher caught her gaze and smiled before leaning down to listen to something a pretty little brunette said.

She sighed, unable to hide her disappointment.

"Dare I hope that sigh means you miss me as much as I've missed you?"

Primrose almost dropped her lemonade as she spun around.

"Leonidas."

She blinked at him, trying to focus her eyes suddenly filled with moisture.

"Happiest of birthdays, Primrose."

He took the glass from her hand and set it on the table before wrapping his arm around her waist and steering her to a quiet corner behind a potted ficus.

"You're here." She had a knack for stating the obvious tonight. "Why aren't you on the ship?"

"I couldn't leave you, Primrose." Leonidas kissed her forehead. "I thought I wanted a life of freedom to continue my travels, unfettered and unrestricted. But as I walked up the gangway this evening, it struck me. None of that matters if you aren't by my side."

"Oh, Leonidas."

He lifted her chin, searching her face.

"Please tell me you feel the same, little hen. That there is hope that you return my affection in some small degree? That in time, you can come to love me as much as I adore you."

"I do love ye." She wiped a tear from the corner of her eye. "I only wanted ye to love me too."

He gathered her scandalously near, and Primrose didn't care.

"Does that mean you'll marry me?" Emotion rendered his voice throaty.

"Aye." She pressed her mouth to his. "I'll marry ye."

The orchestra struck the first notes of the next dance just as a longcase clock chimed midnight.

"Join me in a minuet, my love?" Leonidas's tender, reverent smile nearly caused moisture to pool in her eyes again.

"I'm not very adept," Primrose confessed.

"I am. Quite exceptional, in truth. I'll teach you." His grin proved contagious, and she returned his smile.

Primrose permitted him to lead her onto the dance floor, doing her best to disregard the stares and whispers as people realized Leonidas hadn't sailed to Greece but partnered *De la Chance's* Scottish bookkeeper for a minuet.

Leonidas bowed, and Primrose curtsied.

Across the room, Fletcher winked before bursting into laughter.

"Why is Fletcher so happy?" Primrose asked, glancing over her shoulder as she stepped and dipped.

"Because, my darling, he's been playing matchmaker all along. He knew we were perfect for each other."

She smiled up at him. "We are, aren't we?"

EPILOGUE

Athens, Greece

JULY 1829

Standing on Philopappou Hill and holding his fourteen-month-old son, Leonidas pointed to the Parthenon, aglow with the setting sun's vibrant rays. "That building is called the Parthenon. It's famous for having no right angles or straight lines, Thaddeus. The temple was built for the goddess Athena."

His blond-haired son made an appropriate sound of approval and reached his chubby little fingers toward the impressive structure. "Mine."

Chuckling, Primrose clasped her son's tiny hand. "I fear our son has much of his father in him."

Thaddeus giggled, his dark blue eyes like Leonidas's bright with excitement. He patted his mother's face, then Leonidas's chin.

"Not just his father, my love. His remarkable mother too." Leonidas wrapped his other arm around his wife's shoulders and dropped a kiss on her bonneted head. "How are you feeling?"

He lowered his attention to Primrose's slightly rounded belly. Their second child would arrive in late autumn. They sailed for England next week, for as much as Leonidas relished his travels, his children would come into the world on English soil where their doting grandparents and numerous aunts and uncles could fuss over them.

"Perfectly well." She made a face. "I'm pregnant, not ill."

"Duly noted." Leonidas dropped a kiss on her nose. "I'm not surprised your wayward cousin decided to make Greece his home. If he ever sets foot in England again, his life wouldn't be worth two groats. A person doesn't welch on a debt that size and get away with it."

"True. Besides, after they seized Chesley's house for partial repayment, he had nothing to come back to. Nevertheless, I never want to see him again." Resting her head against Leonidas's shoulder, Primrose sighed. "I'll never tire of seeing these ruins or imagining how they were built. Or wondering about the people who erected them."

After honeymooning in the South of France, Primrose had also fallen in love with traveling and proved a valuable asset on their excursions. She contributed thoughtful and intelligent perspectives, which Leonidas included in their travel books. As a result, the journals had become even more popular, especially with women.

"Where to next?" Leonidas asked. Naturally, they would have to wait until the new babe was old enough to travel safely, but there was nothing to prevent them from planning their next adventure.

'Italy," she said firmly, tilting her head upward. "We still haven't seen the Roman ruins in Verona, Pompeii, or Herculaneum."

"Italy it is, then." Leonidas took her elbow and turned them toward the pathway leading to their waiting carriage. "I shouldn't be at all surprised if Cassius doesn't want to join us again. I think he'll always think of Italy as his second home."

"He's always welcome. You know I adore your family, although it's quite overwhelming when everyone gathers." Grinning, Primrose carefully stepped over a large rock. "In a wonderful way. I missed not having a large family."

"Well, the Westbrook clan is about to increase again." Leonidas lifted Thaddeus onto his shoulders. "Mother's last letter revealed Adolphus, Lucius, Althelia, and Fletcher are expecting little ones. Naturally, Mother and Father are over the moon."

"Splendid. More cousins for our children to play with." She flashed him one of her triumphant smiles, which caused the world to stop for a fraction. "I think I want at least six children."

"I eagerly anticipate the making of our offspring." Leonidas gave her a wicked grin.

A pretty blush colored her cheeks, but Primrose, being Primrose, merely arched an eyebrow. "I know you are trying to shock me, but I quite enjoy that part of marriage too."

To think, Leonidas had nearly forfeited this happiness. What a fool he'd been.

They reached the carriage and climbed aboard for the journey back to their lodgings. Thaddeus fell asleep almost at once, and Leonidas settled his son across his lap. Drawing Primrose against his side, he whispered into her ear, "I love you, my heart."

"I love you too." She raised her radiant face to his. "No matter what happens, where we go or what we encounter, what trials or celebrations life brings us, our love will carry us through. Now kiss me."

And Leonidas did. All the way back to the hotel in Athens.

I hope you enjoyed MINUET AT MIDNIGHT,
If you'd like to leave a review please
scan the following QR Code.

SCAN HERE TO LEAVE A REVIEW FOR
"MINUET AT MIDNIGHT"

Keep reading for a FREE PREVIEW of
KISS A RAKE A MIDNIGHT
Book 7
Chronicles of the Westbrook Brides Series...

FROM THE DESK OF COLLETTE CAMERON®

Thank you for reading **_MINUET AT MIDNIGHT_**. I hope you enjoyed Leonidas and Primrose's story. In an age when a young woman wasn't always allowed to choose her husband and women were often prostituted against their will, Primrose faced two very real challenges.

Fletcher offering her a position as a bookkeeper would have been highly unusual but not impossible. Women slowly began to make inroads in male-dominated occupations, demanding their voices be heard. As history tells us, most men were not receptive to the change.

I'd also like to address Primrose's inheritance from her maternal grandmother. Often, a husband assumed control over his wife's possessions, properties, and monies. Not always, however. Women learned to include specific language and terms in their wills that protected future female descendants.

The Scottish cant used in this story is accurate for the era. I tried to include enough to make the story authentic without making it difficult to read. One other minor detail I'd like to address. I researched the expression "welch on a debt" and wanted to reassure my readers that according to etymologists, there is no concrete evidence that the term is derived from the Welsh people.

Hugs,

Collette Cameron®

Kiss A Rake At Midnight

FREE PREVIEW

BOOK 7 ~ CHRONICLES OF THE WESTBROOK
BRIDES SERIES
KISS A RAKE AT MIDNIGHT©

De la Chance Social Club
London, England

JULY 1827 – EARLY MORNING

As was Fletcher Westbrook's wont, he walked through his social club's now silent and empty rooms with a cup of strong coffee. Tonight, like every other night, the place would teem with glittering guests eager and, in some cases, desperate for a few hours of entertainment.

Caution and wariness tempered the sense of pride that accompanied these daily inspections. Someone had slipped a threatening note beneath his office door last night.

The first such secret message in months.

"Bloody, sodding hell."

Fletcher swore beneath his breath before blowing on the scalding, sweetened brew and taking a bracing gulp. Nothing suspicious had occurred since last March when Torrian Westbrook, his cousin and a private detective, had apprehended the offender responsible for setting two fires, as well as sabotaging and vandalizing Fletcher's enterprises and sending other ominous letters.

The culprit, Mike Prescott, a low-end gaming hell competitor, hadn't appreciated Fletcher's scruples or losing elite customers to the classier, and quite frankly safer, establishment. Prescott had grown careless, hence his apprehension and imprisonment.

As Fletcher stood in the card room with its dozens of round tables, black Italian marble fireplace, and the occasional cobalt blue and gold striped damask settee, he pondered this unwelcome and unfortunate turn of events. He honestly believed he'd put that troublesome annoyance behind him for good.

Until last night.

His half-brother, Leonidas, and the only Westbrook besides Fletcher and their cousin Torrian Westbrook, who knew the whole situation, believed the harassment was over too. So much so the deliriously happy scoundrel had married Fletcher's new Scottish bookkeeper and currently enjoyed a honeymoon in the South of France.

Perhaps Fletcher had grown lax—let his guard down too soon.

But why shouldn't he have done?

Convicted of attempted murder, arson, and a half dozen other crimes, Prescott rotted away in Newgate.

One thing was for certain.

He couldn't be behind this latest episode.

So, who was?

Perchance, Prescott hadn't acted alone as he vowed, and his accomplice had become emboldened once more.

Mouth tight, Fletcher searched his memory for unfamiliar faces when he'd made his final surveillance of the club last evening, just before midnight. The mental inventory did little good. New club members were as numerous and common as pigeons in London.

What set *De la Chance* and his other establishments, *Ivories & Aces* and *The Emporium Theater,* apart from other gaming dens and men's clubs was Fletcher's strict, unrelenting vetting of members as well as absolute intolerance for known cheats, rakehells—*present company excluded, of course*—and randy men on the prowl making overtures toward Fletcher's female employees.

He employed over twenty of the best bodyguards in London to ensure the women remained unharried and the premises were as impenetrable as a cloistered virgin nun behind convent walls. Yet, somehow, someone had managed to not only sneak onto the grounds, but they'd found their way undetected to the private quarters on the club's other side.

Unlike many gaming hells, his upper rooms weren't available for liaisons with bit o' muslins on his payroll. Fletcher never had and never would employ prostitutes.

It must've been a guest who breached his inner sanctum.

But who?

Why hadn't one of his security team seen them?

Fletcher's nape hair stood on end, alerting him that he wasn't alone.

Slowly, he rotated toward the card room's entrance, prepared to defend himself with the ugly knife sheathed at his waist. Upon recognizing the small form sauntering through the opening, adorned on either side with heavy royal blue draperies held in place by a thick gold silk cord, he blew out a relieved breath.

Sean Kenney, a perpetually cheerful, if somewhat small and frail Irish lad of all work, gazed around the room with the chairs overturned on the tables that he was tasked with returning to the floor each morning. Unlike most of the club's other employees, Sean and a few others who tended to more menial tasks weren't required to wear all black.

Today, his delicate features wan, the lad seemed tense and distracted.

Nevertheless, he touched two slender fingers to his ever-present flat tweed cap.

"Good morning, sir. Howya today?"

"I am well." Physically, yes. But unrelenting worry niggled in the back of Fletcher's mind. He must find the culprit before things became dangerous once more. He took another sip of coffee. "Yourself?"

He'd learned long ago that when he took a genuine interest in his personnel, not only did they work harder, but Fletcher could, with a great deal of accuracy, determine which of them would become loyal, long-term help. Consistency among his employees proved essential to keeping his establishments running smoothly.

What he couldn't determine at this moment, however, was Sean's age, though if Fletcher hazarded a guess, he'd suppose the lad was in his late teens. Perchance sixteen or seventeen.

Small for his age, likely due to malnutrition, the youth often conducted himself and spoke like someone older and more mature. His eyes often held a world-weary glint, and fine lines sometimes bracketed his mouth, suggesting he'd experienced much hardship in his short life.

Fletcher rubbed his nose with his free hand.

Reading people had come naturally to him for as long as he could remember—nearly his entire life. The ability was as ordinary as breathing. Much like his interest in medicine had been, which had compelled him to become a physician, only to leave the field disenchanted and haunted over a decade ago.

He'd always admire and respect the individuals who made the profession their life's work. For him, the heartache of watching infants and children die despite his best efforts took a toll that seared his mind, scarred his soul, and left him drowning in defeat. It nearly drove him mad or to the bottle, hence his departure from the vocation before becoming an ape-drunk lunatic.

His expression downcast, Sean shifted his feet and covered a wide yawn.

"The truth is, sir, I'm knackered. My sister kept me up most of the night. Kimber's sick with a nasty cough."

"I'm sorry to hear that, Sean." Fletcher scratched the back of his neck. "Does she need a physician?"

Sean hesitated for half a second before shaking his head.

"Nae. I think it's just a summer cold. I left broth and a tonic. Paddy promised to keep an eye on her." Sean raised a thin shoulder beneath his much too-large black coat. "Forgive my rattling. I'd best crack on."

"Paddy is your brother?" Fletcher also made a point to learn something about his employees' families—those that had families. Many didn't, and it was truly sad knowing they had no one except fellow employees who often became their surrogate family.

"He is." Strong and wiry, Sean pulled the gold velvet

cushioned ebony chairs off the closest table with practiced efficiency. "Turned twelve last month. Kimber is almost eleven."

A wonder the two children hadn't been forced to find jobs as was the usual practice among the lower classes—probably due to Sean's diligence in providing for them.

It couldn't be easy for him.

Had Fletcher ever seen the lad without his coat or hat?

Even in July, the boy wore a plaid muffler around his neck.

In medical school, Fletcher had taken a few psychology courses. He suspected the boy's outer garments acted as protection from more than the elements.

"Did you know I used to practice medicine?" Fletcher finished his coffee and set his cup on one of the tables. "I could look at your sister if you wish."

Impossibly paler, Sean turned huge dark-blue eyes fringed with such lush lashes that women might become jealous.

"No, sir. That wouldn't be right. I know how busy you are. I'm sure she's on the mend already."

Fletcher understood Sean's distrust. Likely ashamed of his living quarters, the lad also probably didn't have a penny to spare to hire a physician. The boy had no doubt learned the hard way that favors often came with strings attached.

Perhaps Fletcher would give the lad more responsibility, requiring a pay raise. Though he hadn't been at *De la Chance* long, only since the end of April, he performed his duties with diligence and cheer.

Mayhap he could tend to the hats, cloaks, coats, and other items for the members? Currently, a maid did so, but profoundly shy, Sally preferred working in the kitchen.

Sean would require a uniform for his promotion, of course.

An advancement was something to consider.

Fletcher had permitted Bernicia Dough, the head cook, to send leftovers home with the boy since he supported himself and his two younger siblings. Sean never mentioned parents, and Fletcher could only assume there weren't any, whether due to death, abandonment, or perhaps incarceration.

Or perchance the children had fled an abusive home as Primrose McKessick—now his brother Leonidas's wife— had done. Sadly, that often proved the case in London's seedier neighborhoods, where poverty, unemployment, and alcohol often led to violence.

In any event, sending along food and other supplies wouldn't put Fletcher out of business. The world was cruel to orphans without resources.

"Good morning, Mr. Westbrook. Sean." Fred Brindlecombe, the concierge, poked his head around the corner before continuing to the front counter without waiting for a response.

Smiling, Fletcher patted the boy's thin shoulder and couldn't help but notice his fine bones. He was much frailer than he let on and undernourished too.

Fletcher made a mental note to tell Mrs. Dough to add extra bread, cheese, meat, and milk to the supplies she sent home.

"At the very least, I can have Mrs. Dough prepare her infamous tincture and a poultice." When Sean opened his mouth to protest, Fletcher shook his head. "I shan't take no for an answer, and if your sister does not improve, promise me you'll allow me to look in on her."

Though Fletcher no longer practiced medicine, he could diagnose perfectly well and obtain and pay for a physician if the child needed one.

"Yes, sir." Though Sean nodded, his guarded expression revealed he had no intention of accepting the offer. Nonetheless, Fletcher would persist for the child's sake and his staff's lest the illness prove contagious.

Fletcher turned to leave but pivoted back toward the boy.

"Sean? What time did you leave last night?"

Most people never took notice of the boy, moving about the club like a silent shadow. He might've seen or heard something untoward.

Tilting his face upward, Sean scratched his head.

"About ten, I think. Maybe a little earlier. It was just after the fancy gent in the red coat arrived. The one with a ruby the size of my thumb in his neckcloth."

"Lord Huxley?" A self-important dandified coxcomb if ever there was one.

Artemus Fogwell, the Viscount Huxley, and his wife's presence had been a bit of a surprise. Huxley, the pompous windbag, had shown a decided interest in *De la Chance* several months ago—well over a year ago, in truth —but last night was the first time he'd graced the club with his presence until closing.

Surely, it was a coincidence that an ominous letter appeared afterward.

Wasn't it?

Fletcher made a mental note to apprise Torrian of that interesting detail.

"Notice anyone suspicious wandering around the private quarters?" Fletcher planted his hands on his hips.

"Sorry, sir." Sean shrugged again, causing his coat to brush the tops of his knees, one of which bore a neatly stitched patch. "But I left through the kitchen like I always do."

Of course Sean had. So he could collect the leftovers and the biscuits Mrs. Dough baked for the youth and his siblings.

"Very well." Fletcher narrowed his eyes, skimming his focus over the boy.

Perspiration dotted Sean's cheeks.

The lad didn't look at all well.

"Are you feeling quite the thing, Sean? I shan't dock your pay if you need to go home and rest."

"Not a bit of it, sir." Sean pasted a bright smile on his pallid face as he placed chairs around the tables. "You can count on me."

Morry Chandler, Fletcher's head of security and second in command, strolled into the main gaming salon, his expression inscrutable. Wiry and bearing a scar on his forehead that paralleled Chandler's right eyebrow, Fletcher trusted him implicitly.

"A word, Mr. Westbrook?" He slid the boy a brief glance. "Privately."

That didn't portend well.

Hopefully, Chandler might have information about the mysterious leaver of threatening notes.

Fletcher nodded as he crossed to Chandler.

"Do let me know if you see or hear anything out of the ordinary, won't you, Sean?"

"Aye, sir." His cheeks unnaturally flushed, the boy ducked his head.

The last thing Fletcher needed was for the lad to spread whatever ailed his sister and quite possibly himself amongst the other employees. Despite Sean's reluctance, wisdom decreed Fletcher ought to take the boy home and check on his sister.

Yes. That was what Fletcher would do—right after finding out what Chandler couldn't or wouldn't say in front of the boy.

I hope you enjoyed this FREE PREVIEW of
Kiss a Rake at Midnight
Book 7
Chronicles of the Westbrook Brides Series.
If you'd like to keep reading
please scan the following QR Code.

GIGGLES ARE GUARANTEED
COLLETTE'S CHERIS READER GROUP

If you love to chat about all things romance-book related and enjoy taking part in fun and engaging live events, contests, and giveaways join **Collette's Chèris VIP Reader Group,** my exclusive private book group on Facebook.

Giggles are guaranteed!

Hope to see you there,

Collette Cameron®

Please scan the following QR Code to join:

GIGGLES ARE GUARANTEED

YOU ARE CORDIALLY INVITED TO JOIN
COLLETTE'S CHERIS
VIP
READER
GROUP

ALSO BY COLLETTE CAMERON®
BLUE ROSE ROMANCE® LLC

COLLETTE CAMERON'S®

COMPLETE BOOK LIST

CHRONICLES OF THE WESTBROOK BRIDES

A Romantic Opposites Attract Mystery & Suspense

Family Saga Regency Romance

Moonlight Wishes and Midnight Kisses — Bonus Novella

Midnight Christmas Waltz — Book 1

Mission at Midnight — Book 2

The Midnight Marquess — Book 3

Holly, Mistletoe, and Midnight Snow — Book 4

The Wallflower's Midnight Waltz — Book 5

Minuet at Midnight — Book 6

Kiss a Rake at Midnight — Book 7

Unmasked at Midnight — Book 8

DUKES COME CALLING

A Sensual Marriage of Convenience

Regency Historical Romance

FOR THE LOVE OF AN EARL (Wicked Earls' Club)

A Humorous Aristocrat and Wallflower

Regency Romance Adventure

Earl of Wainthorpe — Book 1

Earl of Scarborough — Book 2

Earl of Keyworth — Book 3

Earl of Renshaw — Book 4

HEART OF A SCOT

A Passionate Enemies to Lovers

Scottish Highlander Historical Mystery

Romance Adventure

To Love a Highland Laird — Book 1

To Redeem a Highland Rogue — Book 2

To Seduce a Highland Scoundrel — Book 3

To Woo a Highland Warrior — Book 4

HIGHLAND HEATHER ROMANCING A SCOT: CASTLE BRIDES

A Passionate Enemies to Lovers Second Chance Scottish Highlander Mystery Romance

Wishes and Wonder — Book 9

A Yuletide Highlander — Book 10

SECRETS OF SCANDALOUS LADIES

A Romantic Class Difference Forced Proximity

Regency Romance with Aristocrats

A Lady, A Kish, A Christmas Wish — Book 1

No Lady for the Lord — Book 2

Love Lessons for a Lady — Book 3

His One and Only Lady — Book 4

Never a Proper Lady — Book 5

Lady Tempts a Rogue — Book 6

THE CULPEPPER MISSES

A Humorous Wallflower Family Saga

Regency Romantic Comedy

The Earl and the Spinster — Book 1

The Marquis and the Vixen — Book 2

The Lord and the Wallflower — Book 3

The Buccaneer and the Bluestocking — Book 4

The Lieutenant and the Lady — Book 5

THE HONORABLE ROGUES®

A Second Chance Redeemable Rogue

and Wallflower Regency Romance

A Kiss for a Rogue — Book 1

A Bride for a Rogue — Book 2

A Rogue's Scandalous Wish — Book 3

To Capture a Rogue's Heart — Book 4

The Rogue and the Wallflower — Book 5

A Rose for a Rogue — Book 6

'Twas the Rogue Before Christmas — Book 7

A Rogue Worth the Risk — Book 8

USA Today Bestselling author Collette Cameron® is renowned for her captivating, humorous, and heart-warming Scottish and Regency historical romance novels. With over 65 published titles, over 1.4 million books sold around the world, and multiple writing awards to her credit, Collette is a well-known author in the world of historical romance. Readers love her witty and relatable characters including daring rogues, dashing scoundrels, and the strong and spirited heroines who capture their hearts. From the rugged highlands to the refined drawing rooms of Regency England, Collette's novels will transport you to another time and place, where love and adventure are just a page away.

Collette's Sweet-to-Spicy Timeless Romances® are the perfect escape for readers looking for romantic escape, poignant inspiration, engaging humor, and entertaining stories.

Based in the Pacific Northwest, Collette is surrounded by the lush greenery and rainy skies that inspire her writing. She dreams of one day splitting her time between the Pacific Northwest and Scotland. In the meantime, she indulges in her love of all things cobalt blue, dachshunds, chocolate, and of course, crafting her next historical romance.

Blue Rose Romance® LLC
PO Box 167
Scappoose, Oregon 97056 USA
collettecameron.com

If you haven't joined Collette's exclusive mailing list scan the folloing QR Code to sign up!
You'll get access to exclusive content, sneak peeks,
contests, giveaways, and more...
(P.S. No spammy stuff.)

Follow Collette on social media.
Scan the following QR Code: